THE PIRATE
Princess

Janice Vis

THE PIRATE PRINCESS

ISBN-10: 1-897373-75-9
ISBN-13: 9781897373-75-0

Printed by Word Alive Press
131 Cordite Road, Winnipeg, MB R3W 1S1
www.wordalivepress.ca

WORD ALIVE PRESS
Just Write!

To my friends, who thought this was the coolest thing ever.
To Anieta, the most eccentric person I know.
To my family, who encouraged me the whole way through.

And most of all,

To God,
through whom all things are possible.

Chapter 1

Mist hung in the air as the ship traveled between the narrow passageways of the damp cave. Dim light trickled through a small hole in the cave roof. A mouse scurried along the sidelines of the vessel. The whole place seemed eerie. It was completely still, as if time had stopped. The only sound that could be heard was the constant breathing of the sailors and their captain. Not even the soft lapping of the waves was audible.

The ship slowed. It was a good thing, however, for a large rock stood in the vessel's path. The boulder did not bother the captain, for they had arrived at their destination. Nothing needed to be said, for the sailors knew well what was expected of them now. The ship neared the shore. As the vessel pulled up to the rock, the anchor was dropped. It did not take long for the ship to be secured.

These sailors were both known and addressed as pirates, but that was not completely correct. For although their country, Mayblea (May-blee) specialized in ships and navies, the only activity they did that resembled that of pirates was the uncovering of treasure.

"All right, men. Let's hurry this up." Karielle stepped off the *Diamond*, waiting for her assistant, Andrew, who incidentally was also her cousin. Although she had captained the ship alone for but a few months, she had accompanied her father on missions since childhood. This was her first, and by far most important, treasure hunt. Before starting this expedition, she had searched the lands of Mayblea for over a year seeking the map that had led her here. The tension made the expedition exhilarating.

"Let's go, Captain Kari!" Andrew said with excitement. To the lady, however, her cousin's excitement was childish. It was true that Andrew was rather immature—and never serious, to say the least. An expedition like this never brought her any humour until the mission was accomplished. Perhaps this was just as well, for the mission was dangerous enough. But when it was over and no harm had been done, maybe they could find something humorous in it.

As she started off towards their greater objective, Karielle motioned for two of her loyal sailors to follow her and Andrew. She wished to walk without noise. In such a silent and still place, Karielle hated to break the quiet. Even the sound of their feet softly hitting the rock floor was unpleasant to Karielle. Her cousin obviously did not see it that way, though, as his constant chatter filled and echoed off the cave walls. This annoyed Karielle until she felt obliged, for their own personal safety, to shut him up.

"Andrew—" she started. However the chatterbox was quick to respond.

"What's wrong, Captain? No sea serpents in sight, no sharks, no storms, couple mice, but you're not afraid of 'em, are you?"

"No, Andrew, I'm not, but if you dare open your mouth again unless absolutely necessary, I'm going to send you back to the ship." Andrew glanced back at the *Diamond*, only ten metres behind them. Still, Karielle knew that they had only about five more to go until the first turn toward their destination.

Five metres, as it is known, does not take long to cover. When Karielle stopped at a small opening, the two sailors did the same. However, Andrew, being as oblivious and ignorant as he was, kept walking.

He had made it an additional five meters when Karielle called out to him. "Andrew, what are you doing?" Instantly coming to a complete halt, the first mate turned around to meet Karielle's annoyed eyes.

"Oh, right," he said, immediately going to join the sailors and Karielle. When the foursome was all together, they looked at the opening about a half meter above the rock ground. The hole was much smaller than any of them had imagined it would be. It looked dark and uninviting. Andrew looked extremely hesitant as he gazed into the black opening.

"We'll have to crawl," one of the sailors said, finally stating what everyone had been thinking. Karielle, being a captain who always leads her crew, slowly went in first. As Karielle squeezed into the space she silently pitied the two sailors, who would have a much more difficult time since they were much broader than she. Following her was Andrew. Finally, the two sailors entered the cave within a cave. They crawled, sometimes being forced down to their stomachs, for a few minutes before coming to a decision. The opening split into two more small caves. As they approached the fork, the cave widened considerably, so Andrew crawled up beside his captain. The two sailors still remained behind.

Karielle turned toward her first mate. "All right, Andrew, here's your turn. I wanted to bring the map, but you told me you had it memorized. Which way do we go, right or left?"

"Well, I don't really know right or left. I just know that if we have the choice to go forward, we always should," Andrew replied.

"Andrew!" Anger was creeping into Karielle's voice. She knew, as all good captains did, that with one wrong turn they would be lost forever. They needed the correct turn, and there was no going back. She should have expected her cousin to mess something up.

"If we all die today, it is your fault. I'm never going to trust you with anything again!" Karielle declared. She adjusted her body so she was sitting on her shins. Glaring at her cousin, who seemed deep in thought, she wondered why she had even bothered taking him. He hadn't been any help.

"After careful consideration, I have decided it would be better if we lived. Even though if we were gone, there would be fewer mouths to feed, there would be less money to feed with. Since we find treasure and create money, it would definitely be better if we lived," Andrew said. Karielle rolled her eyes. Her first mate was on his first treasure hunting expedition and already considered himself an expert at the task. Now he was talking like he thought of himself as a high philosopher. The two sailors had a hard time controlling their laughter at the first mate's philosophical ignorance so Andrew would not hear them. However, failing, Andrew glanced back, upset with them.

"Disrespect!" he exclaimed to his cousin. He glared back at the two sailors.

"Since when did you deserve respect? They can laugh all they want. You're an idiot," the teenager stated plainly. Then shifting to more important matters, she looked again at her cousin. "Now, are you sure you don't know which way we are supposed to go?" Karielle asked, hoping Andrew had somehow remembered.

"Right. I don't know, right just seems right to me. I don't remember the map, but right just hits me as right." Andrew started to head right. Karielle stopped him. He looked at her peculiarly.

"Andrew, do you know what the Pirate's Code says in Rule 258 part 3?" the captain asked.

"No, but who cares?" Andrew said, the confusion showing in his eyes.

"It says this," Karielle said, reciting the passage she had referred to:

"A pirate's code states it clear,
Right or left, death seems near.
The fool will go to the wrong,
He will ignore the pirate's song.
For right seems right to him now
But soon to him, death will bow.
The wise will know left is right.
The wise will avoid the entire plight.
Follow the fool,
Ignore a pirate's rule,
And meet your death.
But with the wise, go to the left,
And avoid a tragic death."

"And I suppose you're the wise," Andrew said sarcastically. He still felt his instincts were more correct that those of his captain's. As a norm, Karielle would have gone his way just to prove him wrong. But this was different. Lives were at stake. One error would force them to take their final breaths.

"I'm wise enough to have memorized the Pirate's Code, which you haven't a clue about. Come on, we're going left," Karielle stated. He waited a moment, and then Andrew decided to go with his latter impulse, which was to follow his captain. Besides, refusing his cousin would be classified as mutiny, and therefore he would be taking the risk of being hung. That was one thing Andrew could do without. He enjoyed living.

Karielle crouched lower to the cold rock as the small cave narrowed once again as she headed to the left. Andrew slipped behind her again. The two sailors followed obediently, thankful that they were heading the direction that their trustworthy captain had chosen, not the obnoxious first mate. Occasionally, there would be a fist-sized hole in the cave roof. This allowed a small amount of light to filter through. The light comforted the foursome as they crept closer to their destination. Feeling her salty sweat run down her face, Karielle kept pushing on. They had been traveling much longer than they had expected, and she secretly wondered if Andrew had been correct for once in his life.

Again she was forced to crawl on her stomach, and Karielle was stunned that her ancestors had been able to make a living by doing this. Her first mission was already making her uneasy.

It was but fifteen minutes later when the captain rammed her head against a cold, hard rock covered by the black darkness. Karielle again felt a liquid run down her jawbone. As the liquid touched her mouth Karielle realized that, contrary to the first time, this was not sweat. It was blood. Her head aching, Karielle felt defeated. Turning back to look at the cousin who was disguised by the darkness, she leaned back on the rock that blocked their path.

"I'm sorry," she apologized quietly. Certain they should have gone right like Andrew had suggested, Karielle wondered why she had even followed the Pirate's Code, written by their ancestors so many years ago. Putting all her weight on the rock that blocked their pathway, Karielle buried her face in her hands.

It was unusual for the teenager to cry so freely. Not only was she bold, but she was also strong in both character and spirit. Had it been only her in such a predicament, she would have faced the death she was certain awaited her with bravery. But the thought of ruining her cousin and two loyal sailors was more than she could handle. Grief overcame her. But as Andrew sat there, still not taking anything too seriously, he heard a noise that caused his spirits to jump beyond what they had been before. He heard a creak.

"Karielle, wait! Something's happening!" he told her with excitement.

Unsure of what he meant, Karielle resumed her weeping. She didn't even bother to listen to what Andrew was saying. She assumed that it was nothing more than nonsense. Suddenly, the rock that Karielle was leaning on gave way, and she abruptly fell crashing into a pile of gold coins beneath her. Her blood still trickled slowly out of her scalp.

Opening her eyes, eighteen-year old Karielle Blackbird found herself staring upward into a large rock room, with millions of pin holes in the roof that let the day's warming sun through. The rock room was large, and full of the precious and valuable.

"The Forgotten Treasure," Karielle whispered to herself. Andrew, excited and cheerful as always, leaped down into the room of jewels and coins. The sunlight reflected off the shining treasure. Karielle couldn't see the floor of the cave, for everything was covered in coins. It was truly a beautiful sight, not that Karielle cared extensively about the money they had found, but they had succeeded in their mission.

"You were right, Karielle! We made it! Look, it's all here! The Forgotten Treasure!" Andrew's face was filled with joy. He twirled around a few times before stopping. "The Forgotten Treasure, why do they call it that?" the first mate asked, plopping down in the middle of a pile of coins. Burying himself in them, he looked at Karielle. At first Karielle wondered if he was too joyful and obsessed with the treasure to listen to her, but then dismissed the thought and answered his question with one of her own.

"Do you really want to hear the story?" Karielle asked him.

Andrew answered immediately. "Of course I want to hear the story! Come on, tell me, Captain!" His eyes were wide. He was like a small child asking about a fairytale.

"Alright, alright," Karielle said, attempting to calm her cousin. She motioned with her hands for him to be quiet. Then she started one of the tales she knew so well. "We are from the island of Mayblea, located in the Great Sea. As you already know, there is another island in the Great Sea. It is Euriko (Yor-eek-oh), our enemy who you hear so much about."

"I know that," Andrew told her, anxious for her to get farther into the story.

"Anyway," Karielle started again. "You probably also know that Mayblea and Euriko were once one country. They were ruled by a single good and fair king. When the king died, he went against the tradition of giving his whole kingdom to the eldest son. Instead, he gave Mayblea to his eldest son and to his daughter, who was his youngest. She was Princess Lydia. He had two other sons. They were given Euriko.

Mayblea did better than Euriko. The eldest had the most military training, so Mayblea had the strongest military. Because the daughter was also ruling the isle, her traits came out also, such as religion, beauty, graciousness, and a love for nature and its Creator. Instead of sharing in Mayblea's prosperity, one of the Euriko kings became jealous and killed his brother, starting a plot against us."

"Yeah, yeah." Andrew rolled his eyes. "I know all that. You know, how Euriko launched a surprise attack on Mayblea and they met defeat. Ever since then, we've been enemies. How Euriko treated its citizens terribly, and many fled to Mayblea at night by boat. How Euriko is enemies with anyone but themselves, and fire upon any ship that is not theirs. How we are only enemies against Euriko, and therefore only fire at their ships, not any others. How because of our practices and strong navies, we are known as pirates. Sure, I've heard that part of our history before. But what's that got to do with anything?" Andrew recited Mayblea's history like a memorized Sunday school lesson.

"Right, but when Euriko made the attack, they first hit one of the royal mansions. Unprepared, Mayblea was unable to stop them from looting this castle. Princess Lydia had a special jewel in that mansion. It is the only one of its kind and was called the Lydeen, after her. She was devastated and was sure it had been stolen. But after they fought off Euriko and examined the mansion, they found the Lydeen right where it was supposed to be. Euriko had taken everything else—but had forgotten that precious stone. Princess Lydia's older brother then decided to hide the jewel with other valuables from the king's treasury. So, actually, the Lydeen is the forgotten treasure. All this other stuff is just extra. He sure put a lot of treasure with it, though, more than I expected to see."

Andrew's eyes widened, confirming her statement.

"Captain, where is the Lydeen? How shall we find it in all this treasure?" one of the sailors inquired.

"Well, the king put the Lydeen inside the old Euriko king's skull. We went through a lot of trouble to find that map, so we're not leaving without the jewel. Come on, look for a skull," Karielle told him.

Carefully, the two sailors and Karielle searched the room. It was difficult, for the room was large. The first mate was too busy rolling around coins to bother to join them. It was the fact that it was Andrew who found the skull that made the whole situation ironic. In his rolling around, he managed to roll over and uncover the ancient skull. He looked at it closely, then picked it up.

"Hey, Karielle, I found the skull. But there's no jewel in it. Just this piece of paper," Andrew told her, waving the floppy paper in the air. Confused, Karielle headed over to him. Examining the skull intensively, Karielle came to the only possible conclusion.

"It's been stolen," she said.

"What?" Andrew exclaimed. "How could someone steal it? And what's the note for?"

Karielle looked at Andrew before answering. "The note must be from the one who stole it. I don't know how they got to it, though, for we were the first to find the map. There is absolutely no possibility someone else found the map before we did. I wonder how they got it."

"Well, maybe the king decided to keep it. How do you know it's been stolen?"

"Why would the king do that? And see this chip in the eyes Andrew? And over here, the skull has been damaged. It's a sign of struggle. A jewel would be pretty hard to get out of here. But whatever, what does the note say?" Karielle asked her cousin.

After examining the lettering for a few moments, flipping the page sideways and upside down, Andrew gave up. "I can't figure it out," he admitted. He handed it to Karielle, who also had to confess that it was not legible in the room they were in.

"Well, let's get out of here, men," the captain said.

"How?" one of the sailors asked, confused.

Karielle glanced around the room while answering. "This sounds confusing, but the map told us that there is a way to get out of here besides the way we came in, but you can't get in from the outside unless it has been opened from the inside," the captain explained.

Andrew's face twisted. "That does sound confusing."

"Here! I think I found it!" one of the sailors exclaimed. With all the strength he had, the sailor pushed rock, only to find it hadn't budged.

"No, that's not it," Karielle said. She walked over to the wall and ran her fingers over it. The sailors were already trying another rock, which was just as unsuccessful.

The princess, determined to find the way out sooner or later, went to one of the rocks that formed the wall and tried to move it, but nothing happened.

"This may be harder than I first thought," Karielle said.

"Whew! This is hard!" Andrew said, even though he hadn't done a thing yet. He leaned up against the wall in supposed exhaustion, and suddenly a rock from behind him tumbled down and splashed in the water.

Excitedly, Karielle began her orders. "Andrew, find the ship and guide it to this opening. We'll load the treasure and then get back to Mayblea to examine the note. Hurry!" And, as she was the captain, her orders were carried out.

Chapter 2

"Princess Karielle, you have arrived back safely!"
A wealthy noble came back to greet Karielle
Blackbird and her crew after their voyage. The stillness of
the cave was gone, and the ship was safely in the Mayblea harbour.
However, Karielle always found that her identity seemed to change
once she stepped off her ship, the *Diamond*. When on the ship, she was
a bold, ruthless pirate. When off, she was Mayblea's princess again, the
well-educated beauty of the isle. Karielle was not sure if this was to her
liking, but certain things in life were unchangeable. This was such a
thing, so she did not fight it.

But on or off the ship, Karielle always had her sword strapped to
her back. The sword had been a gift from her father twelve years ago,
on her sixth birthday. Throughout these twelve years, Karielle had
learned to master it. Everyone knew that the princess could best anyone
with her sword. Years and years of practice had paid off. It was at this
time that the Mayblea princess reached to her back and drew it. Feeling
its handle, both familiar and comfortable, Karielle swung it in the air
several times. For those present, the action seemed rather pointless, and
perhaps it was, but Princess Karielle, the royal lady and heir of
Mayblea, was a mysterious one. Everyone knew this. Karielle was

often the subject conversed about around the dinner table. The princess was respected, but still a cause for confusion. Karielle couldn't say she minded her reputation, though.

The princess looked up to see another approaching. His steps were long and his body figure was that of a fifty year old man, which he was. He smiled brightly at the sight of the princess.

"Uncle William," Karielle addressed the man who had just joined the noble who had greeted them. William was her father's sister's husband, or Andrew's father. "Andrew has a letter, a note which needs to be examined immediately by our royal scribe. You should probably take him there, or else he might very easily get sidetracked from his duty." Grinning widely at how Karielle had mentioned his son, William did as Karielle said, knowing it was for the best.

The princess waited a moment to make sure her ship was secured. Her sailors were very efficient and swift. She smiled inside. They had been trained well. Then she turned toward the palace and quickened her step. It was beautiful spring day, and Karielle was glad.

In a matter of minutes, Karielle joined her uncle and cousin by the royal scribe. His ability to make out handwriting that seemed illegible to anyone else was one talent that Karielle was amazed at. Although the scribe was gifted, he was definitely not good-looking. His hair was a greyish-blond that showed his age. His teeth were yellowish as well, and seemed overgrown. His face was fleshy, and full of wrinkles that made him look older than he really was. Still, many things would be harder to manage without this man, so the princess was more than grateful for him and all the work he did.

"I must say, this is quite a challenge," the scribe said, biting his lower lip in thought.

"Can you make anything out?" Karielle asked. The scribe nodded slowly. Releasing his lip from his large teeth, he read out part of the letter he could understand.

"*I, Sir Linden Rummbon have been wronged. The captain of our ship, the first king of Mayblea, had Fredrick II take my job as first mate...*" The scribe's voice trailed off. "He seems to grumble on about how the king made a foolish decision and he would pay. Hmmm..." The scribe looked intently towards the bottom off the ancient page. "*If*

11

you have found this note, I greatly apologize. It was not your mistake but the filthy king's. I helped him hide the Lydeen, but when he was not looking I stole the jewel before we enclosed the room. The jewel has been hidden in a place one would never expect. Not in Mayblea, not in Euriko. It is somewhere far away. I have not made a map. The only place where you can find the location is in my personal journal. Signing off, Sir Linden Rummbon."

"Linden Rummbon... I have heard that name before. Read it someplace, I suppose," William noted. Karielle still stood thoughtfully, wondering what her next move should be.

"Well, I'm sorry Princess Karielle. It looks like your Lydeen is lost forever," the scribe sympathized. Sauntering around the room, Karielle had still not spoken a single word. She seemed deep in thought, which she was. This seemed strange to the two men, who exchanged glances of bewilderment. What was this princess up to now?

"You know what, it's not gone. I'll find his diary. I'll sail across the Great Sea. The Lydeen is not lost forever! It belonged first to Mayblea, so it will belong to Mayblea in the end! Come on, Andrew." Karielle started for the door with a unique boldness.

"Where are we going, Karielle?" her cousin inquired as he started to follow her.

Without turning around, Karielle answered with determination. "We're going to find out what happened to Sir Linden Rummbon. Now, pick up your feet." The princess obviously had made up her mind, and once she had, no one could change it. In the past, some had tried, but failed miserably.

Following her out of the room, Andrew glanced behind him to see his father with the scribe conversing about something or other. Andrew wasn't sure why this struck him so strangely, since many castle members and nobles discussed the headstrong princess. It was in a good and honourable way most of the time. Perhaps it was the sight of his well-combed and decently dressed father beside the aged scribe. But anyhow, this struck him as strange. Andrew glanced once more at the two before closing the large, heavy wooden doors behind him. Karielle was quite a ways down the corridor already, and since Andrew was rather uncertain of precisely where they were headed, he quickened his pace to catch up with his cousin.

"Come on now, Andrew, don't be so slow!" Karielle called across the corridor to him. Hurrying even more, Andrew soon caught up with Karielle. He did wonder what the big rush was all about, though. He did not see her reason for moving so quickly. The Lydeen had been hidden for generations. A few minutes wouldn't cost them.

"Just a question Karielle, but where are we going?" Andrew asked, feeling absent-minded, not that it was anything new.

"To the largest royal library, of course!" Karielle acted as though her answer had been obvious. The royal library would have made sense, because the records of all the nobles were within that large room. The Mayblea palace was immense, and the scribe had currently been on the west side. The library they were heading to was on the east. There was, of course, more than just a single library, but they were headed for the largest one, because Karielle did not want to miss even a morsel of information.

The palace was lovely, like any true fairytale castle would be. Built of white brick, it glistened in the sun. From the outside, the castle appeared to have only six stories, but in reality it had twelve.

The castle also had twelve castle towers, and six balconies. The rooms numbered just under twelve hundred, sitting at 1189. The castle was gigantic and beautiful. Often, Mayblea natives had tried describing it to others, only to fail; it was too difficult to describe such exquisiteness to one who had not see it. Ironically, the only word that could describe it was *indescribable*.

Corridor after corridor, Karielle finally stopped at a large set of mahogany doors that were carved cleverly and decorated brilliantly with flowers and vines. With satisfaction and determination, Karielle took hold of the knob and turned it. The door opened easily, without as much as a squeak. Stepping into the palace library, Karielle looked upon mountains of shelved books. They towered above her. In fact, there were about three whole stories of books lining walls and balconies.

"Come on!" Karielle called to Andrew, who was looking nervously into the room. The reason for this would go unanswered into all eternity. Even Andrew did not understand his reasoning. This annoyed Karielle and partially angered her. He did not see or feel her urgency, and so she decided to leave him.

Slowly, Andrew closed the door behind him. Glancing back at the library, he decided that it wasn't so bad after all.

"Come on, let's find what we need. Anything about Sir Linden Rummbon will work. Hurry now, will you!" Karielle tried to instil some enthusiasm. She headed toward the history section. Andrew, knowing nothing about the library whatsoever headed for the fantasy books. When Karielle saw this, she was about to call out to her cousin, but decided against it, since he would not be much help anyway. He would do better being out of the way where he couldn't constantly annoy her.

Karielle continued her search in the history section, but was unsuccessful. There seemed to be no records of Sir Rummbon. Andrew, on the other hand, was quite excited. He was in the middle of a fiction novel about a young boy with the power to make fiery arrows. But as Andrew remembered why he had come to the library, he started to return the book to its original place. However, a moment before he did, he noticed something toward the back of the shelf. It would have normally been hidden by the book Andrew was currently holding. Out of curiosity, something Andrew had too much of, he reached in and took hold of it. Pulling it out and replacing the fiction book, he turned his attention to the object.

It was a small, worn book, a journal, to be exact. The cover was made of leather, and was a faded burgundy color. The bottom right corner looked as though it had been scorched in a fire. Opening it, Andrew wondered why he had chosen this over an enticing fantasy, until he saw a name he recognized. He saw the letters L-I-N-D-E-N R-U-M-M-B-O-N. This was his journal! It held the answers Karielle was looking for, and now lay in Andrew's hands.

Andrew's brain went a million miles per hour as he thought, *What should I do with it? What could I do with it?* Then it dawned on him. He did what any sane person would do.

"I'll show it to Karielle!" he exclaimed to himself. Perhaps his decision seemed slow, and perhaps it was, but either way Karielle saw Sir Linden's diary.

As expected, this event came as a great surprise to Karielle. Her cousin had actually been helpful. This alone was stunning, but the fact that he had found something so important was simply astonishing. The journal meant a lot to Karielle, and she was anxious to look inside it. It would be the key to the discovery of the Lydeen.

Rushing out of library, Karielle, followed by Andrew, came to a sudden halt not five meters from the door. Through Karielle's anxiety over the journal, she had forgotten a very important asset—where were they going?

"Where should we examine this?" Karielle asked. Such an inquiry made her feel absent-minded, rather like her cousin. When such a comparison flashed through her mind, Karielle felt extremely humbled.

"Hmm… how 'bout the study?" he suggested. Such a suggestion to Karielle's question made him feel important. Andrew prized the feeling he didn't have very often.

"Not a bad idea, but which one should we go to? There is one on each of the twelve floors," Karielle noted.

"Well, there are also six libraries!" Andrew said, with a bit of sarcasm. His ego showed his wit, a wit that was not often expressed. Of course, it was not often expressed because it was not often there.

"Good point, but this one was the best, and the largest. But for a study, it need not be a large one. Let's go to the nearest one. There's one a few hallways away," Karielle said. She turned to Andrew. He was aimlessly staring at the wall. Karielle was glad he was being awkwardly dimwitted again, for being as useful as he had been in the last five minutes was contradictory to the real Andrew she knew so well. Now, regaining the determination she had upon entering the library, she headed off to the study. Walking quickly, the princess wished to arrive as soon as possible.

The study was large enough, though not half as large as the library. The walls were decorated with portraits of the royal family. The first one was of Princess Lydia and her older brother. The paintings continued until there were two portraits of Karielle. They were smaller than the rest, for she was currently a princess, not a king or queen. Another picture would be hung when she came to rule. The first painting of her was when she was six. In it, she was holding new sword, which was strapped to her back. The latter picture was one painted only a few months ago. At six, she was adorably cute, and at eighteen she was downright beautiful.

The door of the study swung open as the regal princess and her cousin Andrew entered the room. Sitting down at a table, they opened Rummbon's journal carefully. Andrew flipped to the first page and started to read with great enthusiasm and hand gestures.

"Andrew, flip to a different section of the book. This is all about him being made first mate. We want to know about when he had just been relieved of the job," Karielle told her cousin. Andrew did as she had instructed, but then decided, probably wisely, to let Karielle look for the secret. This surprised Karielle, for Andrew was not usually one to let someone else take such a thrill away. She was pleased, however, for she would rather trust herself than Andrew to find such an important secret.

"Okay, he's been replaced... he's mad..." Karielle continued to flip through the journal. Her eyes brightened as she read a certain page. "*I have stolen the Lydeen. This was the purpose of the king's journey, and now it is ruined. I have sailed a great distance to find an awfully splendid hiding place for it. It rests in a nation far away. It is in Prancera. It is hidden in the castle treasury. I told one of the maids who saw me to leave it there, that it was the correct spot for it. I do not think she believed me, though. If she stole it, I really don't care. The people from Prancera think Mayblea is a fairy tale, so it really wouldn't matter what she did with it.*"

Karielle stopped. Prancera was quite a distance from Mayblea, and she knew that before she traveled to such a distant place for a treasure, she would need to study more about it. Karielle sat there for a long while. She was in deep thought, and while her heart told her to continue to pursue the Lydeen, her mind went in the other direction. Heaven knows where Andrew had gone to.

Time passed. Perhaps it was only minutes, but it could have been hours, maybe even a whole day. But when Karielle did rise from her

16

seat, she had made one firm decision. The princess would follow her heart. She was going to study Prancera, organize a crew, achieve her parents' blessing, and uncover the Lydeen. The thought that perhaps the maid had taken it was disturbing, for then it would be much more difficult to trace, and she would have to take it from the family who had it, and they would have no idea where it had come from. They would consider Karielle's action theft. Still, perhaps the maid had used it for payment of some kind. That would be even more disturbing. But despite the potential difficulties, Karielle was stubborn and headstrong. No matter what had happened to it, she was certain she would find the precious jewel.

Chapter 3

Researching Prancera was not a simple task. In the whole Mayblea castle, there was very little information regarding the faraway nation. Most of this was due to the fact that it was so distant. There had been very few expeditions, and therefore little was known about the place. Perhaps the worst factor was the lack of information on the sea conditions from Mayblea to Prancera. Karielle was a wise and qualified sea captain, but trips that proceeded into the unknown without knowledge were extremely dangerous. Deciding to take her research elsewhere, Karielle started out to the house of Professor Mason Maddson. The professor had been Karielle's geography tutor when she was young. Geography had fascinated her, interesting every ounce of her being. Some thought that this might have been a factor that led the princess to her interest in sailing.

Karielle stared out into the horizon a few acres north of the palace. Opposite the direction she was heading in was Castle Village to the south, which the Mayblea castle also sheltered. It was the capital of Mayblea, but its size didn't live up to the name. It was rather like all the other tiny towns located in Mayblea. But Karielle did not dwell on that today. Rather, she thought solely on her destination.

The house of Professor Maddson was dainty. It sat rather crookedly atop a hill. The house was not large, containing only two rooms. The bottom floor contained one room, while the top floor contained the second. Because of this, the house was quite a bit higher than it was wide. The roof shingles had originally been painted an olive green, but had worn to greyish brown over the years. It had only one window, which was framed with the same greyish brown color. In front of the house, a flower garden blossomed with the strangest possible flowers. It abounded with orange and yellow dragon snaps, and a bright yucca had grown to almost five feet, towering over the small periwinkles that covered the ground under it. An interesting hoya plant had sprung up, growing and consuming the west wall. The pungent aroma was so strong it almost brought tears to Karielle's eyes. The house was so small, and the plants so vivid, that it was as though the plants had taken the house captive. But the plants were good, for they brought life to the home. Without them, the house would look older than the seventy-year-old professor that lived there.

As Karielle stepped inside the small home, a shrivelled, gnarled man looked up from a colossal book. He smiled. He wore glasses almost a centimetre thick. The lenses were perfectly circular and covered a good portion of his face. He stood up to greet his former student. It amazed Karielle that he could still move at all. However, the professor was fairly strong, although that was completely contradictory to his physical appearance.

"Hello, Professor!" Karielle greeted. "How are you doing this fine day?"

"Aye, aye, fine as always!" the old man responded cheerfully. "Now, what has brought you here?"

Karielle paused a moment, unsure if she should explain her situation. Eventually, she simply asked, "Do you have any information on Prancera?"

A strange look passed over the old man's face. It was excitement, like that of a child who had finally got to open a Christmas present after staring at it for ages. It was also that of concern, wondering if Karielle could really accomplish what was ahead of her. It was as if he knew what was ahead, knew what was to happen. For a minute, he looked thirty years younger and his skin seemed to glow. But it only lasted a moment, and then he was ancient once again.

The old man squinted his eyes, thinking intently. "Let me check."

Karielle had seen it a thousand times. The professor grabbed his meter-high ladder, leaned it on the bookshelf, and stepped up, went through his books, occasionally drawing one out, blowing the dust off, reading the title, and putting it back, shaking his head.

Finally the professor stepped down from his ladder.

"Sorry Karielle, I can't help you. Prancera is so far away, nobody bothers to write on it. Maybe you should someday." The professor cackled at his attempt to humour. Karielle realized that it would be better for her to make her exit now, thus eluding any further awkward moments.

"I'm sorry, professor, but I must be going now," the princess told the elder man. He looked up at her with wide eyes. Karielle expected a protest, for this old man never wanted her to leave, but she was surprised at his response.

"Yes, I suppose you do. Well, be off then! Have a jolly day!" the professor said. Karielle was confused. If she didn't know better, she would think he wanted to be rid of her.

And with that, Karielle turned and left. Although she was disappointed that the professor hadn't been much help, she understood that neither his lack of books about Prancera nor his lack of taste in humour was anything he could be blamed for. Therefore, Karielle headed back toward the palace empty-handed. He had seemed rather strange, though.

What Karielle was unaware of was that the professor had been staring at her out of his window as she headed back to the palace. He squinted his eyes with emotion and shook his head slightly. He turned toward the sky and whispered something unknown. It was as unknown as his secret was to Karielle.

Upon her arrival at the palace, Karielle was greeted by her mother, Queen Tamilia Blackbird. Tamilia seemed concerned for her daughter, not that it was anything new. She was seated on a decorated bench near the palace's front gardens. Karielle sat down next to her.

Tamilia wore a baby blue satin dress. Her crown was not large, but still beautiful. A simple line of pearls draped her neck as her only necklace. She also wore jewelled earrings. Neither her dress nor her jewellery was large or any fancier than it needed to be. Her dark hair was pinned back in a neat bun. Someone who had just encountered her might easily mistake her for a lesser noble. But when Karielle compared her mother's attire to her own, she knew for sure that the nobles of Mayblea did not pride itself in riches.

Karielle wore a satin dress as well, though hers was pink. Her sleeves ended just below her shoulders with a frill. The only decoration her dress had was silver embroidery on the bottom half of her skirt. She wore a silver bracelet, which was tight against her wrist. This matched her silver necklace, which was tight against her neck. Her slippers were also silver. She wore no crown, but instead sported a string of circular silver plates that rested on top of her head. Her black locks fell down on her shoulders. Her green eyes glistened with beauty. Her oval face and fair complexion only added to her loveliness. Perhaps this was strange, for Karielle was rarely as gentle and mild as her attire would suggest. Naturally, her sailing attire was different, and probably matched her character more.

"How are you doing, Kari?" Tamilia addressed her daughter by her rarely-used nickname. "You seem to be busy lately."

"I am," answered Karielle. "Since the Lydeen is in Prancera, I've been studying Prancera a lot. When I'm ready, I'll assign a crew and sail off."

Her mother shook her head knowingly. "Oh, Kari, you're so like me. You're so determined, so stubborn. But Prancera is quite a ways away." Tamilia spoke the truth, but Karielle was confused. She had never described her mother as overly determined or stubborn. Her mother had always been a graceful, perfect queen in Karielle's eyes. The other thing that surprised Karielle was her mother's knowledge of Prancera. Despite the fact that her mother had only mentioned it was a long way to travel, Tamilia knew nothing of sailing or geography. Prancera was barely ever mentioned, so the fact that her mother even knew it existed was shocking.

"You're confusing me mother," Karielle turned to Tamilia. Her gentle eyes showed her bewilderment.

"Whatever about?" asked the queen.

Karielle explained, "As far as I know, you're not stubborn at all. The other thing that confuses me is how you know anything at all about Prancera."

Her mother grew serious. Karielle had never seen her so solemn.

"Do you want to hear the story?" her mother asked.

Karielle shrugged her shoulders. "Sure."

"Okay, sit back, because it will take a little time." Tamilia grinned again. Leaning back, she sighed before beginning.

Tamilia was sixteen. She was the beautiful, well-educated daughter and only child to the king of Prancera. Therefore, she was its heir. She had finished her schooling, and was ready to face her life as Prancera's future queen. This was until her parents decided to marry her off. Since Tamilia had a vivid personality and was a headstrong teenager, they figured she would appreciate a knight in shining armour more than a royal noble.

Her parents held a contest, in secret of course, and whichever knight won would become Tamilia's fiancée. One knight, Sir Walters, was stronger than the rest. He won. Later on, Tamilia found out about this, but at the time she knew nothing. Then her parents tried to play cupid, finding ways to create romance by making them sit together at royal meals, letting Sir Walters take the princess to dances, and forcing them to spent time together.

Tamilia hated Sir Walters. He kept on trying to force himself on her. But the princess was strong. When her parents refused to cancel the engagement, Tamilia began to rebel. She sat in her room for days on end with Trudy, her best friend and personal maid, as her only companion.

But that was not all to the story. Before this, Tamilia had discovered the secrets of the Mayblea and Euriko pirates. Most thought they were fairytales, but Tamilia knew the truth from a number of sources, including children's books that claimed to tell true tales of pirates.

It was just after she met Sir Walters that she discovered something else. Timothy Blackbird, a handsome, trustworthy Mayblea pirate, was hiding in Prancera on some sort of mission. It turned out that his mission failed, but before he realized it, he had fallen in love with the Prancera princess. Tamilia had fallen in love with him, too, for that's the way good romances go.

While she was fighting with her parents about Sir Walters, Timothy was preparing to leave for Mayblea again. When Tamilia came to visit him in secret the night of his departure, he asked her to come with him and marry him there. She accepted his proposal, and they ran off to Mayblea together, where he was the king and ruler.

Karielle was stunned. She had never known about her mother's past before. She had always assumed that her mother was a Mayblea noble before marrying her father. This was a new concept to the princess.

"I didn't know any of this," Karielle told her mother truthfully, her face still marred in surprise. Although it was stunning, she didn't feel that her mother had rejected her by keeping it a secret, as Tamilia had once feared.

"Maybe I should have told you sooner. This really affects your future life, too," Tamilia noted. Though she said it like it had just occurred to her, she had thought of it many times before.

"How does this involve me and my life?" Karielle inquired of her mother.

"It's quite simple. I was the only relative and bloodline of the Prancera royal line. Therefore, I was the heir. But I was more than that. I was the only heir. There is nobody else to hold my place. Right now, there is probably a family ruling outside of the law. It's part of the tradition. When a royal line ends, another family takes over. But the line didn't end. Everyone probably thinks I'm dead," the queen explained to her daughter.

"That means I'm the heir. The true princess of both Mayblea and Prancera is me," Karielle said, realizing her position. Her mother nodded.

"You have a decision to make now. You either forget I ever told you, or you go to Prancera for the Lydeen and claim your throne." Now it was Karielle's turn to nod. Yes, it was true. Karielle really did have an enormous choice to make.

Karielle decided to think and pray about it. The decision she had to make was not an easy one. She went inside the palace slowly, thinking hard about her next move.

But as Karielle closed the heavy wooden door behind her, she popped her head back out.

"Mother?" she started. Her mother turned her head toward her only child. "That story… about you and dad. That's a true love story."

Chapter 4

"I'm going." Karielle's mind was made up. "I'm going to Prancera for the Lydeen and for the throne that should have been my mother's."

Karielle had completed her research. She had decided. Prancera was her destination. Work still had to be done, though. Her crew still had to be assigned and prepared. The *Diamond* still needed to be inspected to make sure it was in shape for such a long journey. But none of that mattered. To the princess, those were details. She was going. That was all that mattered. Everything else would be sorted out soon enough.

She decided to let her mother know first. This made sense, since her mother was the one who had told her in the first place. Her mother was excited and pleased with Karielle's decision. Her father was also cheerful when he heard of her upcoming journey. Everything seemed to be going well for the eighteen-year-old princess.

Currently, Karielle was walking on the wooden dock along the coast of Mayblea. She glanced at her two-mast ship. It looked magnificent as it slowly floated up and down with the waves. It was definitely not the largest ship in Mayblea, but everyone had to agree it was the most beautiful. Her crew had not yet been assembled. She had seriously considered leaving Andrew behind, but he had been her first mate for years. She knew he would be offended if she told him to stay back. That was the only thing she had decided. Andrew would be her first mate, annoying or not.

Slowly sauntering past the *Diamond,* Karielle gazed blankly down the harbour. She was not gazing at anything particular, but rather at the deck as a whole. It was still early morning, so a slight chill made its way up her back. Karielle was accustomed to it. She had never been one to sleep in.

A light breeze caressed Karielle's dark hair, making the locks float up into the air and swirl back down. Karielle grinned. The serenity of the early morning was something she had always loved.

As the sun rose higher on the eastern horizon, more people were beginning to move about. A few sailors checked over the vessels at dock. It was a typical Tuesday morning.

Making her way through Castle Village, Karielle was greeted by several villagers. Karielle greeted them, and was greeted in return with a smile and a kind word. Such was the way in Mayblea.

As the princess walked along the brick streets, she let her imagination wander. Her thoughts to Prancera. Karielle was so consumed in her thoughts that when she strolled around a corner she almost ran into one person she hadn't expected—Andrew.

"I thought you'd still be sleeping. You're definitely not a morning person." Karielle was snapped back to reality instantly.

"I would be, and I'm still sleepy. Man, I don't have any clue how you do it, gettin' up so early," Andrew said. He paused to yawn. "But Mom said somethin' about you making a decision to go to Prancera for your throne, or something like that. She said I should ask if I was yer first mate." Seventeen-year-old Andrew stretched his arms, yawning once again. Karielle wondered how word had gotten around so quickly. It was just yesterday she had alerted her mother of her upcoming journey.

But, deciding to answer the question Andrew had implied, Karielle turned her mind toward the current encounter.

Grinning slyly, she said, "Oh, come on, Andrew! Do you seriously think that after all this time I'd abandon you?" Andrew smiled weakly. He was still tired.

"That's cool. Now, I'm gonna see if I can get a few more hours of shuteye." Karielle's cousin started to walk away.

Still smiling, Karielle called after Andrew. "Sure, you do that. I'll assemble the crew and make all the arrangements myself." As expected, Andrew was beside her in a flash. The princess knew her cousin well. He preferred to be included in all the arrangements that had anything to do with a journey by water. Andrew fell into step with her as they headed toward the palace.

As they neared the castle, Karielle decided to discuss her crew with her father. At such a time in the morning, King Timothy Blackbird would probably be in his personal study, thinking. Karielle knew that even in such a wonderful nation like Mayblea, ruling was not often easy.

Walking swiftly toward her father's study, she motioned Andrew to follow silently. She did not want to disturb her father.

Slowly opening the wooden door, she stepped in. As she had predicted, her father was sitting down with middle and index fingers supporting his forehead, with his elbow resting in the table. He was staring intently at the papers in front of him.

When Andrew shut the door softly behind him, the king looked up at his daughter and nephew.

"Don't let us disturb you," Karielle said gently. She smiled warmly.

Her father grinned back. Of course, his grin was different than his daughter's. His smile was rather crooked. He looked every bit the pirate he was, although Mayblea pirates weren't really pirates at all; they were sailors. But they were known as pirates, so that was how they were addressed.

"You couldn't disturb me if you tried." The king looked lovingly at his only child. Karielle was his precious child, his daughter. He motioned for them to sit down. They did.

"We hope not to bother you. I know you're really busy. But... I was wondering. We're going to Prancera, and I have to assign a crew.

I've never traveled so far. You've been to Prancera. What do you think? Do I need the strong, or the smart? Do I need the experienced, or the young and adventurous?" Her face showed her hunger for her father's wisdom. The king appreciated this. His daughter was smart, but she was also smart enough to know that her father was more experienced in such matters. Her questions showed her wisdom.

"I struggled with this as well when I first went. But nobody had been to Prancera. You are very wise asking me this," the king replied. Karielle blushed at the compliment. Any admiring comment from the king was taken as high praise.

The king continued. "I assumed the waters would be hard. I chose the experienced and the smart. I made it, but not easily. Sailing to Prancera is a long journey. The experienced were older and tired faster. The main challenge will be violent storms, and for that, again, you need strong sailors. Young and energetic sailors are also very helpful, although I had only one with me. You don't need to be extremely experienced to sail through a storm, but you need to be tough and full of youth. Assign the younger sailors, Karielle. You won't regret it. They'll make it through easier."

Karielle was thankful for the advice. She nodded her head, understanding her father's view. She was glad she had come here.

Rising from her chair, Karielle smiled at her father. He had a rugged, but rather striking appearance.

Andrew rose from his chair as well. He bowed slightly. It was at this moment that Karielle realized Andrew had been completely silent. It was also at this moment that she realized his eyes were full of reverence and respect. That was not like Andrew. However, after only a moment of thought, Karielle recognized why this was. Andrew had almost never approached the king before, and when he had seen the king, it was during formal visits by his parents to the throne. Never had Andrew seen the king with anything other than loyal respect. His actions made sense to Karielle.

"You're not leaving already?" The king's inquiry could be taken as a protest.

"We wouldn't want to keep you, and now I know how to assemble my crew," Karielle answered.

"Your majesty," Andrew added, as his first spoken words. He made no indication of a corny joke. Karielle thought this almost humorous, for Andrew was acting as though he was standing before a saint, not a real person.

The king caught this the same way his daughter did. Although he was not familiar with his nephew personally, he had knowledge of what he was like. But he still wished for the two to stay with him.

"You haven't kept me. You probably never will. I don't get to see my daughter and my nephew in my study every day," King Timothy Blackbird noted. Andrew's eyes opened widen at the mention of *his nephew*. Apparently he had never considered himself in those terms. Karielle smirked. Her father grinned.

Sitting back down, Karielle decided to make use of this time. "What do I do if I meet a Prancera ship along the way and they start firing? I could never fire back at a Prancera ship." The princess looked to her father for advice.

Shrugging his shoulders, the king answered, "Very simply. Sail like crazy. Any ship from Mayblea can outrun a ship from Prancera, and the *Diamond* is probably our fastest." Karielle understood this as well.

The king motioned to one of the servants for tea and refreshments for the three of them.

"One more thing, Karielle," the king said. His daughter snapped to attention. "You may run into whales, or maybe even sharks. Don't let them bother you." Karielle had run into sharks before, but not often whales. There were some you could see from the coast of Mayblea in the distance sometimes. Karielle had never seen one close up. This was an experience Karielle was looking forward to.

The tea came, as did some sugar-filled tarts. The king grabbed one, and munched enjoyably. Karielle also took one, chewing on it normally. Andrew was the last to take one. He reached out nervously, and when the king wasn't looking, he snatched one away. Then, as the king turned his gaze toward his nephew, he nibbled on it rather like a mouse. If one was sitting there, they would have had a hard time controlling their laughter, as did Karielle. But shaking her head, she turned again toward her father.

29

"I've studied Prancera quite a bit, and discovered that the best place to dock a ship is at the beach on the west side. We're coming from the northeast, so it might be difficult to go around the entire nation without being seen and attacked. My thought was to find an eastern beach. Where did you dock?" Karielle asked her father.

The king nodded. "There should be a beach suitable for docking on the eastern end. It will not be too difficult for the *Diamond*, considering its size."

Andrew was halfway through mouse-chewing his tart. He probably had some questions of his own, but was too paranoid to ask, or say anything whatsoever.

"When are you planning to leave?" the king addressed his daughter. Reaching for his second tart, he waited for Karielle to answer.

"Two days from now, the seventeenth if possible," Karielle answered. Although she had finished her tart, she neglected to eat another.

The king's eyes shot open. Then, regaining his tranquility, he shook his head. "That's soon! You're just like your mother. Don't worry, that's not really a bad thing. All right, the seventeenth it is. You'll be busy, though. I'll talk to the head chef to see what can be done about your provisions for the journey. Don't worry about that now. Go assign yourself a crew. I take it Andrew is your first mate, once again." The king motioned to Andrew with his hand.

Karielle winked at her father. "We Blackbirds are known for our loyalty."

"Couldn't have said it better myself," the king grinned. Rising from the table a second time, Andrew and Karielle left the king unaccompanied as they departed from his study.

"You were so weird, Andrew!" Karielle giggled when they were back in the corridor. Color slowly rose to his cheeks.

"Well, it was kind of awkward for me, you know. I don't ever see the king so casually," Andrew defended himself. "It was difficult for me to do anything I usually do."

"Well, he's my father, and you don't have any trouble being yourself around me," Karielle reasoned. Andrew realized she was right.

30

He shrugged his shoulders. The red in his cheeks lowered considerably. Not wanting to embarrass him further, Karielle let the matter be. Walking once again down the hallway, Karielle and her cousin strolled along in silence.

Finally, when they were outside the palace, Karielle broke the silence.

"So, who do you think we should assign?" the princess asked her cousin.

"Well, the youthful and strong, like the king said." Andrew was confused as to the reason for her inquiry.

"I know that! I mean, what about names? The crew we had last time worked pretty well when searching for the Lydeen. That was a young crew. Do you think we should just use the same crew?" Karielle asked.

Andrew shrugged. "I don't see why not."

"All right, I'll make it official," Karielle said simply. It made her job much easier. She had to admit that her crew from the last expedition was a good one. She trusted them. They trusted and respected her. That was important when sailing.

Karielle would know.

Chapter 5

"Fire! Fire!"

The fearful shrill ran throughout the Castle Village. A small townhouse was consumed by roaring flames. The fire burned vibrantly like a great lion, consuming its prey. The flames crackled and growled. Screams could be heard from all ends of the small town beneath the great palace. Blankets and barrels of water tried to extinguish the great fire, but it barely weakened. A few brave folk would dash in from time to time to rescue the helpless victims.

Such an event always drew the princess' attention. The midnight cries brought Karielle to quickly dress before rushing down the stairs. The stable attendant gave her a horse, and not bothering to wait for it to be saddled she bolted bareback to the blaze. The horse's hooves clamoured on the brick streets of Castle Village. The horse brayed loudly as the stopped by the flames.

Suddenly, Karielle saw two men emerge from the flames, each carrying a form they had dashed in to save. Both were still alive. Karielle silently thanked the Higher. It was a surprise that they had not been killed. Such fires were deadly.

The first form coughed several times. It was a good thing though, for Karielle knew that coughing was a sign of life. It was a blond-haired female. She eyes opened her eyes and Karielle saw the reflection of pure fear in them.

"Probably about my age," Karielle whispered to herself. The girl coughed a few more times before staggering to her feet. She leaned over the second form, which was a boy of about nine or ten, according to Karielle's guess.

"Nathan! Nathan! Are you okay? Get up, Nathan!" the girl cried to the younger boy. The princess was stunned that the girl still had energy to yell with such volume. Karielle figured that the girl was probably running on adrenaline alone. The boy coughed violently for several minutes. He slowly started to sit up. Resting back down, he breathed heavily.

"He'll be okay," a woman said, kneeling down to comfort the girl. The girl turned toward the woman, with eyes filled with fright. The woman quickly backed off, afraid she had offended.

Suddenly another brave male who had tried to help wounded or harmed, came out with another form, which was man. However, it was the way the body hung, the way the eyes were closed, that caught the princess' eyes. The man was no longer among the living. He hung lifeless in the arms of the one who had tried to save him. It was too late for him. Karielle felt bad for the brave man, for he had risked his life for that of another, but hadn't made it in time.

The girl stared intensely at the form. "Uncle Gregory! Please, Uncle Gregory, don't leave us! Uncle Gregory!" The girl buried her face in her hands, weeping. Her whole body shook. Karielle hung her head. Uncle Gregory, whoever he was, had left this earth forever.

Two villagers came and took the dead off the street, probably to prepare him for burial. The girl turned back to the boy, who was now sitting up. She sat down beside him. Tears still in her eyes, she whispered something that wasn't audible.

Karielle dismounted. She knelt down beside the girl. The girl looked up at Karielle. Her eyes widened. This was expected, since the girl had probably not expected the princess to sit down beside her. The girl probably hadn't even considered the princess to be in attendance.

Karielle smiled warmly. "You should go home to your parents now. You've had a long night." The princess expected the girl to take

33

the young boy to another house, or at least to find their parents, who Karielle assumed to be present among the large crowds, but instead the girl bit her bottom lip and stared at the ground. She slowly shook her head.

"You don't have parents... or a home," Karielle guessed. The girl looked up at the princess. Karielle understood. Of course, she could send them to an orphanage. But despite the fact that they would be well-treated, Karielle knew it would make for a difficult adjustment.

"Come on. You can stay with me tonight," Karielle told the girl. Her wide eyes suddenly became much wider. It was one thing to meet the princess, but quite another to stay in the palace where she lived. However, the girl obviously realized it was the best solution, so she and the boy followed. She looked back at the flaming house. The fire would be out soon. It had been a long night.

On the way to the palace, Karielle asked the girl questions, which were always quietly answered. The girl's name was Cynthia Nelson. Nathan, the boy, was her younger brother. Her mother had died when she gave birth to him, and her father not long after. They had stayed with their uncle since that time. They were not terribly well-treated, but they had been given shelter and food.

Karielle set them up in a spare room across from hers. Cynthia was nervous, Karielle could feel it. But nobody could fault the girl, considering everything she had gone through.

The princess could tell Cynthia was distressed. She could hear her tossing and turning though the night. It would be a long wait for daylight to come, a very long wait of getting twisted in blankets.

When the morning came, an orange sun rose on the eastern horizon. It was a beautiful spring day.

As Karielle rolled out of her bed, she remembered Cynthia. She wasn't quite sure what to do with the girl. She would have kept them with her, but the trip to Prancera was on the day after. She decided to spend the morning meal with the two Nelsons instead of eating at the royal table as she usually did. The Nelsons were already up by the time Karielle went to check on them, but the black rings under Cynthia's eyes indicated that she hadn't slept much.

Cynthia was dead silent. The breakfast of eggs, buttered toast, and a variety of exquisite meat including bacon, ham, and sausage was obviously not what they were accustomed to. Cynthia didn't react except to widen eyes again. Nathan, who was younger by quite a few years, began stuffing himself. The princess could tell the girl was not fond of her brother's behaviour, but was too embarrassed to say anything.

"Do you have any other family at all?" Karielle asked.

"No," was all that Cynthia could manage. The girl looked up and caught Karielle's eyes in her gaze. Her eyes were light blue, glistening in the morning light. Her hair was blond. She was pretty, very pretty, though she was also very scared. Her brother had blonde hair as well, though his eyes twinkled dark brown.

"How old are you?" Karielle inquired. She grinned pleasantly.

"I'm almost seventeen. Nathan is nine," Cynthia responded. Karielle smiled. Maybe Cindy was beginning to open up a bit. She was putting her answers into sentences. Perhaps she was not always so timid.

"No! I'm nine and a half!" Nathan exclaimed between chews. Then, on a more relevant topic, he asked: "What's gonna happen to us?"

"I'm not really sure yet. I would keep you with me, but I'm leaving for Prancera tomorrow."

"By ship?!" Nathan's eyes shot way open. "Can I come? I want be a sailor some day and have my own ship." Nathan was so excited that he dropped his egg halfway to his mouth. The first thought that came to Karielle's head was how ridiculous the request was. But when she looked at Cynthia, she realized it might be worth considering.

"We don't have anywhere to go. It would be a great help if you took him. I'll find work or something," Cynthia said. Karielle shook her head.

"Cynthia," she started. "If I take your brother, I'll take you as well." The words rung in Cynthia's ears.

"Me? What do I know about sailing?" the teenaged girl asked.

Karielle shrugged. "There are other things one can do on a ship besides sail. Cooking, a little bit of sewing and cleaning, they all need to be done. But I'll talk it over with Andrew."

"Andrew?" The inquiry came from Nathan.

"He's my first mate. He's kind of annoying and obnoxious, but don't you mind him. He's also my cousin," Karielle nodded.

The morning meal was finished soon enough. Cynthia was starting to come out of her shell. This was not an easy thing for the teenager.

"Hey, Andrew!" Karielle called out to her cousin. He was walking in front of the burned-down townhouse from the night before. Karielle caught up with him.

"Say, I heard you put up the two people from this house last night," Andrew commented. Karielle nodded. "What are you gonna do with them?"

"You'd never guess, but they want to come with us to Prancera," Karielle answered.

"What? Why would they want to go with us to Prancera?" Andrew asked. His face was twisted in confusion.

Karielle paused. Then she said, "It's not so much that they want to go to Prancera. It's more that they want to go with us to Prancera. They just don't want to be alone here, I guess. They don't have a place to stay."

"I dunno…" Andrew started, unsure about the arrangement.

Karielle smirked. "Wouldn't you like an assistant?" she asked playfully.

"Yes, sir! I mean, ma'am. I mean, yes, I would like an assistant," Andrew stuttered to find the correct wording.

"Nathan would be good for the job. He's ten, young enough to be under you. But he's also old enough to know foolishness is not tolerated," Karielle explained. Andrew liked the idea. She knew he would.

"Tomorrow, at sunrise," Karielle told him. He groaned. He anticipated the departure from Mayblea, but he wasn't so keen on the sunrise part of it.

It was then that Karielle spotted a figure sauntering down the road. She immediately recognized it to be Cynthia.

"Come on, I've got to introduce you to somebody." Karielle urged her cousin to follow her. Quickening her pace, she headed toward Cynthia.

When they were assembled together, the princess made the introductions. "Cynthia, this is Andrew, he's my first mate. Andrew, this is Cynthia, she'll be helping me on the journey." Cynthia smiled. Andrew nodded in recognition.

"You can call me Cindy. Everyone does," Cynthia told him.

"Cindy. I like that." Karielle cocked her head to one side and examined Cindy. The girl pressed her pink lips together. Her cheeks were pink, as they always were. She smiled sweetly. Karielle was surprised at how quickly the girl was making progress, but the princess kept in consideration the fact that Cindy had not been close to the uncle that had died the night before. The girl still seemed hesitant about certain things, though.

"Where's Nathan?" Karielle asked Cindy.

Cindy waited a moment, then said, "He should be somewhere in the village. I'm not quite sure where exactly. He told me he would be back in a moment." The princess nodded. The girl continued slowly. "So... will we accompany you on your journey?" The question seemed distant.

"Yes, you will. Nathan will be Andrew's assistant. You can help me around the ship once in a while," Karielle told her. Cindy let out a sigh of relief. "But," Karielle continued, "you must be ready to leave by sunup tomorrow. We are setting off when the sun is halfway up the horizon. Make sure you are awake. Can you do that?"

"Oh yes, yes!" Cindy reassured Karielle. "We'll be there, I promise!" Cindy said enthusiastically. "Now, if you'll excuse me, I have to go find Nathan. He most likely got sidetracked by something." Cindy headed off to find her brother.

"Pretty creature, isn't she?" Karielle commented to Andrew. When he did not respond, she glanced at him. Andrew had his face tilted down toward the brick street, pretending to kick a rock that wasn't there. A thought came into Karielle's head. She smiled wryly. Then, deciding it was utterly ridiculous, she dismissed it.

"Don't just stand around, Andrew! Let's go see my father to find out if our provisions are settled yet," Karielle suggested.

So off they went.

Chapter 6

Sunrise came. It always seemed to. Heavy dew lay on the ground, which was normal for the spring. The air hung with excitement. This was the day of the great journey to Prancera.

The sailors were present, as was the first mate. Andrew yawned loudly. He rested his exhausted head on his weary shoulder. The captain came out to examine her crew. Satisfied, she nodded to herself.

Among the others present was Karielle's father, who had come to send them off, as well as Andrew's mother, the king's sister. Cindy and Nathan were there just as they had promised.

Before the ship was boarded, Karielle mentioned the two Nelsons who would be going along with the rest of the ship's crew.

"Men!" Karielle said with authority. All the sailors came to attention. "These two will be accompanying us to Prancera. Nathan is Andrew's assistant. Cynthia, or Miss Cindy, as you will address her, is my aid. Respect them as you would me." The sailors seemed to understand.

Karielle and the crew boarded the ship. She overheard two of the men speaking.

"Andrew needs an assistant?" the first said to the other.

"Yeah, to keep his head straight," the second grinned. Both sailors snickered.

The first spoke again. "The princess knows it's probably for the best. She's a smart lass."

"Aye, you speak the truth. Anyway…" The two moved on to a more sailing-appropriate topic. Karielle smiled. Andrew did need an assistant to keep his head straight. She also appreciated the fact that the crew thought highly of her.

The *Diamond* sailed out of the Mayblea harbour. It was as though a graceful dove had broken out of captivity and found its wings. Karielle waved goodbye to her father and aunt, who did the same in return.

"Come, men. Let's get going. We have a long journey ahead of us," Karielle told her men. She glanced back. The harbour was still in full view, but the king and his sister were no longer visible. The harbour slipped away into the distance quicker than Karielle would have thought. Looking around, Karielle noticed that Cindy was not on deck.

"Could she already be in the cabin downstairs?" Karielle muttered to herself. Andrew looked at the princess, thinking she had said something to him. Karielle waved him off. Deciding to check, she slowly started to head town the stairs.

Karielle had insisted that Cindy share her cabin. Usually, the captain had her own private chambers, but the princess had decided to put Cindy up with her. Along with a few other reasons, Cindy was the only other female on the ship. Both were close in age, and the princess felt there could be a valuable friendship blossoming. So despite Cindy's protests of interrupting Karielle's privacy, she had the bottom bunk in Karielle's room.

As Karielle had guessed, Cindy was in the cabin. She was lying on her back across her bunk. In front of her, Cindy was holding an open book. Karielle found that interesting.

"Are you a reader?" she asked. Cindy immediately sat up straight.

"Yeah," she admitted sheepishly. She shrugged her shoulders.

Karielle protested. "Oh no, I didn't mean it that way. There's nothing wrong with reading. It's actually a trait I admire, finding amusement in books. Personally, I would rather swing a sword than read a book, but honestly, reading is a very good thing." Cindy sighed in relief. Karielle was rather confused at Cindy's passion to make a good impression on the princess. She had never seen it before. Perhaps Cindy would lighten up in time.

Returning to the deck, Karielle noticed that the other Nelson was not feeling the least bit out of place. Nathan looked quite excited, running from one side of the deck to the other. From time to time, Andrew would ask the boy a favour, such as to check ropes to make sure they were tight, or to fetch his compass from whichever sailor he lent it to last. Being who he was, Nathan would always "Yes, sir" the request with a formal salute. Andrew always good-naturedly saluted him back. This tidbit of acting always brought smiles to the sailors. Everything was going well.

By noon, the *Diamond* had made considerable progress according to Karielle's calculations. The sea currents were being a substantial help. They had a good wind to use, and sailing had been smooth. Cindy had parted with her book for the time being and was currently walking along the deck. The princess was thankful that the two Nelsons had taken to the sea well, for they would not have enjoyed sea sickness.

"Oh, um… Princess Karielle?" Cindy approached Karielle with a questioning face.

"Cindy, please don't call me Princess Karielle. Just call me Karielle. It's much easier. Don't worry about being so formal," Karielle replied.

"Oh, okay. Karielle, I have a question." The statement was obvious enough to Karielle. She waited for the inquiry, but none came. Karielle cocked her head slightly. It was as if Cindy was waiting for permission to ask her question. Instead of saying anything, Karielle turned her head to face Cindy's. She raised her eyebrows.

Finally, Cindy spoke. "Well, Nathan is really excited about this whole thing. He says that we're making really good progress and we're ahead of schedule. He's also saying we'll be there way sooner that we first suspected. That being as it is…" Cindy struggled to find the right words, "it's still going to take a while, won't it?"

41

Karielle nodded. "Nathan is right. We are making good progress, and we're ahead of schedule. However, it's only been one morning. That could change in an hour or two. Even if we do keep up this pace, the trip will take at least a week and a half. This is not a small bit of water we're covering," Karielle responded. Cindy nodded slowly.

The soft lapping of the water splashing against the vessel gradually grew louder. The salty air was an old friend to the captain. But her senses told her that although sailing was smooth at present, it would not stay that way. Still, the captain decided to dwell on the ship's current good fortune.

Andrew relieved Karielle from navigating the ship. As he started, he realized he could once again use his compass.

"*Nathan!*" he called out to his assistant. The boy, who had been leaning on the railing, looking at the water from the starboard, started to walk over to the first mate. Karielle noticed that he was moving much slower than he had been in the past.

"Yes, sir?" he mumbled with a yawn.

"My compass, go get it from whichever sailor I lent it to. I believe it was Smith," Andrew told the boy.

"Yes, sir!" Nathan replied. He saluted Andrew, but the captain could tell he was weary.

When the errand was finished—it turned out Lutenburg had the compass, not Smith—Karielle approached Nathan.

"Hey, Nathan," she started. The boy's head perked up. "You look kinda sleepy. You've been up since dawn. Why don't you go down to your cabin and rest a while?

The boy hesitated. He seemed to want to go, but was reluctant to leave his duty as Andrew's assistant. This was confirmed in his next statement.

"What... what about Andrew?" The question was expected. The princess grinned.

"Don't worry about Andrew. He'll be fine. He has done without an assistant many times before, not that you haven't been a big help," Karielle told him. Nathan nodded slowly. He started toward the stairs that would lead him below the deck.

Cindy seemed to be keeping company with some of the sailors. Most of them were only a little older than her, so it worked out well. However, seeing that the princess was no longer steering the ship, Cindy started off towards her. In their short period of acquaintance, Karielle had formed a respect for the girl.

However, Karielle noticed that she was not the only one examining Cynthia Nelson. In vane, though perhaps it wasn't, Andrew had also cast his eyes toward the teenager. The same sly thought that had entered her mind the afternoon before came upon her a second time. Yet, as she had been done before, Karielle dismissed the idea as ridiculous and silly.

"Uh, Karielle? Why did you tell the sailors to call me 'Miss Cindy'? I mean, just 'Cindy' is fine with me." Cindy directed her question to the captain.

"It's very simple. You are a guest on this ship. Therefore, you must be treated with respect. They're males, you're a female. It's just a matter of propriety. If you wish for some of them to call you Cindy, then that's fine, but when first entering an atmosphere of men who you don't know, I think you'll agree with me that it's better to start with formalities," the captain explained.

Cindy cocked her head to one side. "That makes sense. Sorry, I was just wondering."

"No apology needed. Questions are always gladly accepted." Karielle smiled. Cindy headed off toward the bow of the ship. Karielle stood there, enjoying the moment.

It was a moment that seemed to crawl while Karielle was savouring it, but once it had passed, Karielle realized how short it had really been. The sun started setting on the western horizon faster than any of the crew on board of the *Diamond* had imagined it would.

Day one was complete.

Chapter 7

The second day passed much like the first, as did the third and forth. However, the fifth day brought events that were more noteworthy.

The sun had been bright the previous days, but on this particular Tuesday, the sun seemed to hide above the dark clouds covering the sky. Fog blanketed everything, everywhere. The wind was a shrilling scream, throwing Karielle's hair to and fro.

It was early morning, but the storm fast approaching them was no secret. The sailors were already fighting the waves. This almost frightened Karielle.

"Err... this doesn't look good, Captain," said Andrew as he walked up and stood beside Karielle.

Karielle rolled her eyes in annoyance. "No duh!" But Andrew had been correct, more than he would ever know. Karielle's breathing became intense. She opened her eyes wide, observing the sea before them. In her whole sailing career, she had never seen such a terrible storm on the horizon. The clouds above her were moving swiftly, positioning the vessel almost directly under the black storm clouds ahead. Karielle bit her lower lip. There were many times when the sea was her friend, but in situations such this, the waters were her enemy, and Karielle was well aware that this would be one hard battle.

"Prepare the men for a hard fight, Andrew," the princess told her cousin. She didn't direct him exactly how he should accomplish this task, but he left her to inform the crew of one thing or another.

Karielle took two steps forward, and then halted. Her green eyes were still fixed on the incoming clouds.

A great crackle of thunder echoed on the waves. The wind was already teasing the ship, threatening to overcome it. The waves splashed violently over the ship's railing. By midmorning, the sky was completely black. The only light that the ship saw was from the blinding flashes of lightning and the dim glow from various lanterns on the ship. The rain, which had been falling for the last hour, was now accompanied by hail. The raindrops had picked up so much force, though, that the hail was hard to distinguish from the rain.

Karielle's icy hands gripped the ship's wooden wheel as a wet chill ran up her back for the thousandth time. A sudden blast of wind flung her tussled hair in her face, blocking the little vision she had.

Another full blast of thunder rumbled in Karielle's ears. The lightning fork landed extremely close to the vessel, bringing screams from several sailors. The first mate seemed to be helping a sailor secure something, but through the blinding gale the captain couldn't be sure. Abruptly the ship's front dipped down into the sea. Splashing back up, the *Diamond* threw Karielle off balance. As the princess hit the hard deck, she felt exhausted, so much so that she couldn't rise right away. But slowly, she did. As she stared in the black, she felt vulnerable, small. Squinting through the rain, she noticed to her dismay that one of the lanterns was slowly losing its security in the rope to which it had been tied.

"Andrew!" the captain screamed through the storm to her cousin, who was near to the burning lantern. "Andrew, the lantern!" Karielle was yelling with all her power, praying that somehow her voice would make it over the winds.

It was clear that Andrew had not heard her words, but had heard something. Looking around, Andrew's head whipped sideways as he saw the lantern. The winds blurred his vision for a moment. The lantern finally lost the rope entirely. Falling ... falling ... falling...

Andrew lunged for the fragile lantern. His hand reached it as it was about to crash. Karielle sighed, momentarily forgetting about the terrible storm they were in. The situation might have proved fatal. Had the lantern crashed, it would have shattered and set the whole vessel up in flames.

Many of the sailors had tied themselves to the ship, securing themselves. But Karielle had refused to, as Andrew had done.

Another booming growl of thunder brought Karielle back to reality. She dashed around the ship, struggling to put out all the lanterns. The captain knew the sailors' jobs would be much more difficult without the dim light, but it was too risky to leave them on.

Karielle was thrown off her feet again as the ship made another fierce lurch. More water splashed over the rails. Karielle felt the salt water reach her feet before easing back down into the Great Sea. As the captain attempted to rise, she was thrown down again. Feeling completely frozen, Karielle straightened her blouse and blue trousers ending at her knees. The princess was well aware that her appearance didn't really matter, since the wind would ruin her clothes anyway.

An earsplitting rip sounded above Karielle. Flinging her gaze upward, Karielle, still sitting down, watched in horror as the wind ripped one of the sails almost straight across. The sail was hanging limply by not much more than a few threads. Karielle rose to her feet.

About this time, Cindy had become increasingly concerned for Nathan, who Andrew had not sent down to the cabins when the storm became more violent. Cindy herself had been thrown off her top bunk onto the floor in pain. The ship was rocking so violently now that reading her novel had become impossible. Yet still, Nathan had not returned to the cabins. Doing what any concerned sister would, Cindy decided to go on deck and bring him down. Reaching for her shawl, Cindy knew it would not be a pleasant experience.

As Cindy stepped onto the deck, she questioned her decision immediately. The wind hit her hard, almost knocking her over. She had been chilly before, but the cold, icy rains made her grip her shawl even tighter. Searching the deck for her younger brother Cindy grew a new appreciation for Karielle and what she went through to captain this ship. As thunder crashed above her, Cindy experienced a sudden shot of fear. The lightning followed a few seconds after, causing a blinding light. Scanning the deck instantly, Cindy finally spotted her brother by the railing, looking every bit as afraid as she was. He was attached to the railing by a single thread, which was much less than what most of the sailors had. Cindy assumed correctly that her brother had wanted to be like them, found a scrap of rope, and simply attached it to the railing.

"Nathan, you are coming below deck, now!" Cindy ordered her brother when she finally reached him. Soaking wet, Cindy hoped her brother would not put up a fight. Her hopes were naïve.

"What? There's no way!" Nathan told his sister, trying to look brave and manly. "I'm staying here! You can't make me leave. I'm attached!" the boy said matter-of-factly, showing her the rope she had already seen.

Cindy shook her head. She would have also put her hands on her hips, but she needed them to clutch her shawl. "You're not attached, not like you're supposed to be. You are not staying here! It's way too dangerous!" Cindy raised her voice even more, half because she was becoming angry and half because the wind was furiously loud.

"No, no, no!" Nathan screamed above the storm. He was acting younger than his age. To Cindy's relief, she spotted Karielle heading toward them. Cindy knew that the captain wouldn't tolerate either of them being on deck.

"What in blazes do you think you're doing?" Her angry voice was louder than Cindy and Nathan's together. "You," Karielle pointed to Cindy. "Get back down to your cabin." Cindy was grateful for the order that was issued to her. She had no desire to be on deck with such a storm. Another blast of wind almost made all three of them lose their balance. Cindy started off to the stairway as quickly as the gale would allow her. She vaguely heard Karielle talk to her brother behind her.

"Go join your sister now!" Karielle ordered the boy. She grabbed a small blade and cut the rope Nathan had foolishly tied in the first place. As the boy started to open his mouth, Karielle realized that this was going to have to happen under protest. The captain, disgusted, grabbed his arm and dragged him below deck.

"What did you think you were doing?" Karielle's rage made tears surface on Nathan's eyes.

"J—J—Just being a sailor!" Nathan protested.

Karielle sighed in frustration. She did not want to be too hard on the boy, yet his actions had been absolutely imprudent.

"Look, Nathan," the captain said, lowering her voice. "You've been a great help. But you are not a sailor. Right now, your main priority should be to take care of your sister, okay? Being up there wasn't right. It was young and immature. If you really want to be someone of respect, you need to stick to your present duties. Understand?" Karielle asked him. Nathan nodded quickly and then disappeared into the cabin his sister had been sharing with Karielle.

The captain enjoyed the security of being below deck for a moment, not that the violent waves didn't toss the ship madly. But without the rain and blinding lightning, it seemed to be calmer. Turning back towards the stairs that led upward, Karielle started up to face the storm.

She would have guessed everything on deck was as it had been, which was not great. When she had gone down, the ship had been mostly under control.

However, when the winds hit Karielle, she saw that Andrew had commanded the men to prepare the cannons. Confused and angry, Karielle fought her way to her cousin's side. The ship was being tossed much worse now due to the lack of sailors trying to control the *Diamond*.

"Andrew, there is no reason for this, and no excuse! Do I make myself clear?" Karielle's voice fought the shrilling wind.

"Karielle, there's a ship out there! We need to be ready!" Andrew explained.

Karielle glared at him and his lack of reasoning. "I don't see any ship, and even if there is, how is it going to attack us in this storm? Mayblea has the best ships. If we're having trouble, what do you think they're having?"

Andrew cocked his head, his hair flying everywhere. "Oh," was all he said. Karielle rolled her eyes. But then a crackling thunder followed a blinding lightning, which lit the sea. But that was not all that lit the darkness, for in the flash of lightning, Karielle saw that Andrew had been right. Indeed, there was a ship, and extremely close to the *Diamond*. The lightning bolt had hit the highest mast on the ship, engulfing the entire vessel in flames. The sight of a ship going up in flames was not a pleasant one. If there had been no rain, Karielle would have been afraid that the flames would take her vessel too, but she quickly realized how ridiculous that would have been, since the ship was not nearly close enough for that. As the ship went up totally, Karielle felt a lingering sorrow. Suddenly, the rain became a drizzle and the wind stopped its teasing. All seemed fairly quiet as the now-smaller waves enclosed the ship.

Then, Karielle spotted a form floating limply on a broken piece of wood. Being a princess, yet a pirate, she did the only thing she could allow herself to do. She threw off her sword, despite confused calls from her first mate.

And she dove.

Chapter 8

D aniel… Daniel White… Prince Daniel White of Prancera.

That was who he was. He knew that. But about the wheres, whys, whats, whens, and hows, he wasn't at all sure. The best he could tell, he we falling in slow motion, with nothing but black surrounding him. Until… yes, there was a sound. It was similar to a voice, yet terribly muffled. And suddenly, Daniel White was no longer in the air. He was on a surface, a cot, he assumed. It slowly came. The noises were voices, but he still couldn't make them out. Then, he realized the why he couldn't see anything but black. His eyes were tightly shut.

He slowly opened them. Fuzzy forms, shapes, and colors were there to greet him back to the world. Slowly, his vision cleared. And then he swore he was looking at an angel. Her light blue eyes, her wavy black hair, and soft, pale face were complemented by rosy cheeks and pink lips. Who was she, this angel?

Finally his vision cleared completely. He was lying on a cot, his face up. A lovely young woman was staring down at him from beside his bedside. She was not an angel, but shared great resemblance to one. A string of white glass beads lay peacefully atop her head, rather like a crown. She wore a snow white blouse with a square neckline.

"Say, Andrew, our patient has awakened," Karielle told her cousin. She stared back at the man who she had been pulled from the Great Sea but a few hours ago. He was examining her closely. The princess giggled. He had dark hair, though not black like hers. His brown eyes had a certain glow, a certain softness to them. Karielle giggled again. Doctoring a foreigner had definitely not been on her agenda, though it was now clear he wouldn't need much doctoring for long.

Daniel stared up at the young man who had now joined the angelic woman. He did not resemble her in the least. He was not tall, though appeared to be due to his lean body and skinny build. His sandy blonde hair shone dimly by the lanterns that lit the room. Suddenly, Daniel realized something else. He was on a ship. Soft rocking was a clear signal of that.

"Where are you from? What's your name? Who are your parents? What about the ship that went down? Are you the captain, the first mate, or a sailor? Do you respect Mayblea? Are you from Euriko? Do you know where you are? How long have you been on your journey? How far are we from Prancera? How old are you? Are you going to answer me!?!" Andrew's seemingly endless questions sent Daniel into a whirlwind.

"Andrew!" Karielle scolded her cousin, who looked up innocently. She continued. "Has it ever occurred to you that he's probably tired, exhausted, and worn out? Maybe this isn't the time to ask a million questions," Karielle told him. Andrew shrugged. Karielle sighed dramatically out of frustration. "Just... just go get Cindy."

Daniel moaned as a sudden burst of pain shot through his head. Then everything turned black.

"He passed out again," Karielle explained to Cindy as they entered the room where Daniel was lying down. "He'll be fine in a few days, though."

Cindy looked at the princess, not sure how to word what she was going to say next. "Why... why'd you do that?"

51

"Do what?" Karielle asked Cindy. "Why did I do what?"

"Umm…" Cindy mumbled before finding the right words. "Like, dive in? Why did you dive in to get someone you didn't know when you weren't even sure they were still alive? I mean, I couldn't do that."

Karielle shrugged it off. "It was the right thing to do. Besides, I've been trained from years of sailing and swordsmanship that it was pretty much the only thing I could allow myself to do," the princess explained. Cindy still didn't understand, and Karielle could tell. But she didn't pursue the issue farther, so Karielle let it drop.

"Where's Andrew?" Cindy asked, changing the subject. "I don't see him here. I thought he returned after telling me you wanted to see me, but I guess not."

"For the better," Karielle told Cindy, her eyes showing her seriousness. "When he," Karielle pointed to Daniel, "first woke up, Andrew started to bombard him, with sixteen billion questions."

Cindy laughed, but Karielle didn't find it humorous in the least. "Just like Andrew," Cindy noted. "Ignorant, totally misunderstanding, and overall just strange!" Karielle had to admit that was a good description of Andrew's character. He didn't mean to be that way, it was just who he was. It was just plain old Andrew.

Karielle wasn't exactly sure what she was to do with her patient, whoever he was. Something about him struck Karielle. She couldn't verify what it was, though.

"Well, anyway," Karielle said, about to continue. However, instead of shifting her gaze to Cindy, the target of her words, she continued to examine the man she had rescued. It seemed strange to call him a 'man,' since he was probably around her age. But Karielle realized that she, being eighteen herself, was no longer the child she had thought she was. The thought rather stunned her, for time seemed to have flown much faster than she expected.

"Well, what?" Cindy interrupted her thoughts.

"Oh, um, yeah, right." Karielle let out a nervous laugh. "If you could stay with him, and doctor him, maybe give him some hot broth or something. For most of the days that would be really great. I'll be with you a lot, too, but I'm still the captain of this ship, and I can't always be here."

"Sure, no problem," Cindy told the princess simply. "I don't have much to do during the day anyway." Karielle nodded. She started to walk away, but Cindy suddenly said softly, "He's kind of, well, you know, striking."

"Striking?" Karielle pretended to be unaware of the very idea.

"You know… striking. I don't know how you'd say it. Handsome, good-looking." Cindy shrugged, trying to act as if it didn't matter. She was quite unsuccessful.

"I wouldn't know," Karielle told her simply before departing the room. Cindy stood there, wondering what she had meant.

Chapter 9

His head still ached and he was still dizzy. But compared to previous days, Daniel White felt fit as a fiddle. He wasn't sure what time it was. All he knew was that he was tired of lying around on his cot, doing absolutely nothing. Daniel couldn't stand feeling useless, whatever his current condition. It had been three days since he first wakened to a face he thought to be an angel's.

Daniel swung his legs off the cot. He struggled to get up. Once on his feet, his head spun even more. Ignoring it, Daniel started toward the cabin's door. Once in the ship's corridor, Daniel was thankful that the stairs to the deck were visible from the door of his cabin. Daniel had no idea whatsoever how this ship was laid out.

Slowly stumbling up the stairway, Daniel enjoyed the scent of fresh air. The captain was out, as were some sailors. Daniel realized, however, that there would be many more people on deck had it been midmorning or afternoon. A captain of a ship himself, Daniel decided it was early morning. The other thing that confirmed his assumption was the fact that the sun had not quite fully risen, though there was full light.

A few of the sailors spotted Daniel as he fully stepped out onto the vessel's deck. Although they started to walk towards him, Daniel saw the angelic lady motion for them to leave him be. She appeared to be the captain of the ship, which was rather surprising to Daniel. In Prancera, a female doing anything more than getting married and having children was unheard of. But he had long since learned that this was not a ship from Prancera. Still, Daniel was the prince, and therefore had been educated as a prince. He had no knowledge of any nation that allowed a female to be anything more than a housewife. He silently prayed that he was not on a pirate ship.

Daniel glanced over at the female captain, who appeared to be headed his way. She didn't look like a pirate, except... Daniel cringed. *Except for the sword on her back,* he thought. But pirates weren't supposed to be pretty, were they? And she definitely had more than her share of looks. In fact, she looked a lot like the portraits of Princess Tamilia, the last of the last royal line. After she had ran away and died, Daniel's father had become the new king, thereby starting a new royal bloodline. Such was the tradition in Prancera. Once one line died, another began. But a new line wasn't allowed to start until the other had completely died off, relatives and all. Otherwise, the new line would be ruling falsely.

"Oh my goodness," Daniel whispered to himself quickly. A thought came to him. What if Tamilia hadn't died? Her body hadn't been recovered. What if this was her? But, no. Tamilia would be much older by now. Might this be her daughter...?

The lady was within vocal range.

"Hey, get tired of lying around in your cabin?" she asked. Daniel didn't answer. He couldn't. He wasn't sure what to say. The female captain motioned for him to follow her. The captain slowly led him toward the stern of the ship. Leaning her back on the railing, the captain cocked her head to one side and examined him.

"I'm Karielle Blackbird, princess of Mayblea and captain of this vessel. Who would you be?" she asked. Daniel then figured out the reason she had led him here. It was well out of hearing range of the other sailors.

"Daniel White," he said, deciding to leave out the fact that he too was royalty and a captain. Then, suddenly, he perked up, realizing what she had said. "You're kidding, right?"

"Kidding?" Her voice failed to mask her confusion.

"Mayblea? You're the princess of Mayblea?" Daniel asked sceptically. All his life he had been taught myths and fairytales about Mayblea and Euriko. But they were just that, just tales. They weren't real.

Karielle laughed. "You're from Prancera. I can tell. Everybody thinks Mayblea and Euriko are make-believe in Prancera and the surrounding nations. Trust me, they're not. Everybody here is from Mayblea."

Daniel was stunned. And yet, something about Karielle made him believe her. Maybe it was her melodious laugh, or the sparkle in her eyes.

"You seem to know a lot about Prancera," he noted.

Karielle nodded. "That's where we're heading now. I studied it, and my mother taught me a lot."

Daniel winced. He had to say something. "Your mother," he started, his eyes locked in hers. "Your mother was, or is, Princess Tamilia, the true ruler of Prancera?" It was a guess, but a good one.

Karielle was shocked. "How did you know that?"

"You look almost exactly like the portraits of her when she was sixteen," Daniel explained. "What happened to her? Why did she run away from everything she loved in Prancera?"

"They didn't tell you about Sir Walters, and my mother's fight with her parents?" Karielle asked. Daniel shook his head. Karielle started again. "Okay. In short, Tamilia, my mother, was being forced to marry Sir Walters, a knight who she detested. Her parents forced her to sit by him, go to dances with him, and so forth. Tamilia started a rebellion against her parents. At the same time, she found out about Mayblea and Euriko from a man who was from there, Timothy Blackbird. It turned out that he was the king of Mayblea, visiting Prancera on some sort of mission. Tamilia and Timothy fell in love. Because Tamilia knew Timothy wouldn't be accepted in Prancera, she later accepted his proposal for marriage and ran off with him." Karielle breathed heavily. Daniel looked shocked, justifiably so.

"So you're the heir of both Prancera and Mayblea?" he asked.

Karielle nodded. "Is that a bad thing?" Her voice was uncertain.

"Well, my father won't be thrilled, but I think it's kind of cool," he explained.

"You're father took over Prancera after they said my mother was dead? That would make you the prince of Prancera. Well, not really, but you know what I mean."

"I wasn't looking forward to it, trust me. I sympathize with your mother. My parents tried to marry me off to a girl, too. We were friends, but we couldn't fall in love. Between the two of us, we've been able to put off marriage."

Small talk was exchanged between them until one question came up from Karielle that changed the direction of the conversation.

"So, was that your ship, the one that went down during the storm?" the princess inquired. She was beginning to like Daniel very much. He was both interesting and charming.

"Yes, I suppose so. I don't remember much, and most of it is fuzzy. The *Dahlia* was a good ship, but no ship from Prancera could come close to surviving that storm." Karielle nodded, feeling sorry for him. To lose a ship, especially one you've captained, was not an easy thing. Daniel continued the conversation. "So, if you don't mind me asking, I wouldn't mind knowing exactly happened to me. How did you find me? How'd I end up here?" he asked.

Karielle paused momentarily. "Well, this ship, the *Diamond*, wasn't too far from your ship. We saw her go down. I spotted a limp form floating on a wooden shaft, so I... well, I dove in, and here you are today."

"You... saved my life?" Although voiced like a question, it was more like a statement of incredulity. Karielle, obviously more than slightly embarrassed, glanced franticly from side to side, left to right.

Daniel, realizing what a spot he'd put her into, simply reached out his hand. She shook it, grateful that she didn't have to answer. She had saved his life, but to put it in those terms rather stunned Karielle.

"Thanks," he whispered. Karielle's eyes met his. They sparkled. She opened her mouth to say something. What it was, though, no one would ever know, because both parties were interrupted by someone far more ignorant.

"Kari, Karielle, Princess Karielle, no, Captain Karielle, I dunno," Andrew called from the other end of the ship.

"Not a morning person?" Daniel asked, rather comically.

Karielle sighed. "You guessed it," she said with a roll of her eyes. But she so annoyed that she could block the giggle that escaped her lips.

Karielle started toward Andrew, who was stumbling around like a drunken sailor.

"Andrew!" Karielle started in a voice filled with authority. "Now, we'll have none of that! Come, you look almost as foolish as you are. Stand up straight!"

Andrew stood up as straight as he could and wearily brought his hand to his forehead for an appropriate salute. Yawning extensively, he mumbled, "Permission to go back to bed and sleep in?"

Karielle almost laughed out loud. Here he was, Andrew, her cousin, nephew of the king, asking to go back to bed. His hair was ruffled. His clothes were wrinkled.

"Go on, you!" Karielle said. She watched Andrew stumble down the stairs. She shook her head slightly. She may be his cousin, but they were more different than black was from white, the sun from the moon. They had often been compared as such.

It was the beginning of Daniel's second week on the *Diamond*. He was stunned at the difference between his former ship and this one. This vessel was much smaller, but also sturdier. Karielle had informed him that the wood the *Diamond* was built from was a special type of white pine. Surprisingly enough, the color of the wood gave the ship a bright, silvery glow. The ship was also incredibly fast as it ripped through the water. Daniel took note of how well the ship was run and organized. It would take twice the crew Karielle had for those from Prancera to sail the *Diamond* smoothly. However, Karielle's organization constantly had the vessel under control. Although he, like Karielle, had been trained in swordscraft since he was he was very young, when Karielle had asked him to demonstrate his skills to her he discovered she was much, much better than he. He had been taking lessons from her the last few nights.

One thing still continued to trouble him. Sooner or later, Karielle would arrive in Prancera. The way the vessel and weather had been cooperating, it appeared that it would be sooner. By that time, Daniel would have seen a major improvement in his swordplay. Karielle was an excellent teacher, and the quick tricks and methods came easily to Daniel. It was completely different from what he had been taught all his life. He was still far from being as good as Karielle, but his newfound skills would be far better than anyone from Prancera.

Daniel was painfully aware, however, that when they arrived at Prancera, he would assist in leading Karielle to the throne. This in itself was not something Daniel resisted. He enjoyed the thought of giving the true throne to the true ruler. Nevertheless, Daniel knew in his heart that his parents would detest the idea of giving up power. Once they had learned he had been a part of it, they would be disgraced. He could see his father's anger already, as well as his mother's tears. He hated disappointing his parents, but Daniel knew the line of duty he had to follow. He fully intended to do whatever he had to in order to assist Karielle.

A fact that was not lost on Daniel was Karielle's beauty. He had never been one for the ladies. It was probably just his character. It was Karielle's character, however, that made Daniel look twice. Naturally, the fact that he had once mistaken her for an angel counted in her favour.

As Daniel scanned the horizon, he knew that his life had changed dramatically since arriving on the ship from Mayblea.

Chapter 10

Hours, days, weeks. The waves still lapped up the sides of the ship. The winds still blew, and the sun still rose. The salty sea air was still Karielle's friend.

"Land ho!"

The words bounced off the sea waves and resounded in the ears of every sailor. All eyes turned toward the horizon, trying to make out even the slight bump. Slipping out a telescope, Karielle scanned the horizon once more. Indeed, there was a bump on the horizon. They were approaching land. Prancera was within their grasp. Karielle could feel the excitement level rising amongst her men. The eyes of the sailors danced as the *Diamond* continued its path. As it cut through the water, the sweet sound of a light breeze rustled the ship's sails.

"You look a little happy," Daniel said as he stepped beside Karielle. "I suppose you're excited to get here."

Karielle glanced over his way. She met his snicker. "Yeah," was all she said. She leaned on the railing, staring at the waters. She hadn't realized how eager she was. Karielle wasn't sure why she was so anxious. Was it for the Lydeen? Was it for the throne of Prancera? Karielle wasn't sure.

"Sorry, I didn't mean to offend you," Daniel said, glancing down.

"Oh no, you didn't. Don't worry," Karielle assured him. She met his eyes and then examined his face. She wasn't sure what he was thinking.

"So, when will we get there?" Daniel continued on a more appropriate topic. He never got an answer, for Karielle didn't hear. She was deep in thought. It wasn't a normal state for the eighteen-year-old. Still, Karielle wondered, wondered about Daniel. But whatever she thought, she knew Prancera was not far away.

And indeed, it was not. The bump on the horizon grew larger and larger. As the ship neared land, Karielle grew more excited. The sailors grew more anxious. Daniel grew more nervous. Karielle inspected the maps once again, confirming a point for docking. Karielle preferred that they not be seen, though it would be impossible. Through her telescope, she could already spot fishing vessels and war boats.

Cindy was also in on the excitement. Although Prancera held no particular interest for her, she was thrilled for no other reason than that everyone else was. Her life had changed drastically since meeting the princess.

"Look! Look!" Nathan hollered. Several sailors turned to examine Nathan's reasons for piping up. "A whale, a really big one! Look, over there!" Nathan shouted once again. This proclamation led the captain to drop her telescope and head toward the boy. Indeed, a whale was dancing amongst the waves. It seemed to be playing with the waters. It was really quite cute.

"Hey look, a whole pod!" Daniel, who had now joined them, pointed to a pack of whales.

"They're Phancerala whales. Beautiful. They are known to be quite rare, though," Karielle noted.

"Fan-ser what?" Nathan asked.

"Phan—sir—al—a. Phancerala whales," Daniel answered for Karielle. Instead, Karielle was staring at Daniel, examining him carefully. Then, when his eyes met her gaze, she looked away quickly, kicking herself inside for allowing herself to do such a thing.

"Oh," was Nathan's single response.

"Excuse me, Captain, but we seem to be approaching land quickly," a sailor interrupted. As Karielle shot her gaze up to the horizon, she recognized how correct the sailor was.

From land, perhaps there approach would have appeared quite ordinary. A vessel was pulling up to the beach. But for the *Diamond*, it was not ordinary. They had come to a new land. Karielle had travelled to many different places during her treasure hunts, but this seemed different. This was an adventure.

Daniel hopped off the ship and onto the sand. This was home for him, and yet their arrival wasn't ordinary for him either. He was no longer a reluctant heir, but a sailor assisting a beautiful pirate. Surprisingly, this felt more right to him. He felt more at home with this bunch than he ever had. He glanced over at Karielle. Why did she have to be so lovely? They were friends, good friends, the best kind, but could they ever be more than that? Daniel shook his head. It was utterly ridiculous.

Karielle had done an impressive job. The ship was not only docked safely, but against all odds the *Diamond* had not been seen. That was important for the mission they had come to carry out.

Nathan jumped off the ship, too. He wobbled a bit. Karielle laughed when Cindy looked concerned.

"You'll feel it too when you get off. Walking on the ship is different from walking on land. I've never seen someone that bad, though. Come on," Karielle urged Cindy, as she too jumped onto the land. The warm sand felt wonderful. Land felt so sweet after such a long journey. Prancera was a pretty country. The beach was composed of fine, soft sand. Beyond that was grass, and although it did not look as nice as that in Mayblea, it was still more than Karielle had expected.

There was not a single cloud in the sky. The sun beat down on the sailors with warm light. A breeze caressed Karielle's face as her hair flew into the air, dancing with the wind. Karielle closed her eyes to enjoy the moment. After only a couple seconds, however, she opened them again.

"What do you think?" Daniel asked Karielle as he walked up to her.

"It's much prettier than I expected, honestly, it is."

"Glad you think so," Daniel responded. He scanned the land he had lived on his whole life. He knew that it was about to change drastically, though perhaps not so much physically as his way life. Daniel still drew a blank trying to come to any conclusions. Was this a good thing, or a bad thing? He wasn't sure.

"Well, what do we do now?" Andrew asked, joining the two. "We're here. What's next?" Realizing the truth in Andrew's statement, Karielle motioned for a young sailor.

"Somethin' you'd be wanting, Captain?" he asked.

"Grab a few of your friends. Scout the area within a kilometre and be back with a report before dark," Karielle told him.

"Yes, ma'am!" he responded with enthusiasm.

"We're setting up camp?" Daniel asked. Although Karielle was silent, her nod was enough of an answer.

"Well, what are we waiting for?" Andrew asked. His eyes danced as he started skipping childishly toward the ship.

"You know, he really confuses me. Sometimes I think I have him figured out, but I'm far from it," Daniel mentioned to Karielle, while still watching the first mate.

Karielle laughed. "Don't worry. I've known him for sixteen years and I still don't have a clue. I've accepted the fact that I'll never understand that one!"

The bright sun slowly moved toward the west. Time ticked on. The sun moved closer and closer toward the western horizon. Karielle began to wonder about the sailors she had sent out. Hopefully, they would be back soon enough.

Any anxiety Karielle might have had was premature. The sailors were back before nightfall, just as they had been ordered. They were completely exhausted. Panting for any oxygen their lungs could grasp, the sailors plunked themselves down in front of a crackling fire.

Karielle looked on from the distance of a few meters. She wasn't sure what to think. Her sailors were strong, and although scouting could be difficult, she had had them do such things before without there being any problems. Deciding to join them, she sat cross-legged in front of the fire.

"Are you guys... okay?" Karielle asked, with both a hint of worry and precaution in her voice.

"Yeah... sorry if... we were... late," one of the sailors said between breaths.

Karielle chose her words carefully. "No, you weren't late. I was just wondering if anything happened out there."

"See, we were all right. At least, until we ran into big trouble," one of the sailors started.

Another sailor filled in. "After about three quarters of a kilometre, I ran into some men. Except they didn't look much like people from Prancera are supposed to look. It turns out there's hundreds of them, and not far from here, either." Karielle's face showed confusion.

"Why would anybody be here if they aren't from Prancera? What kind of people did they look like? Villagers, royalty, what?

"Warriors, all of them. See, one of them, probably a scout, spotted me. He was alone at the time, so nobody else knew. At first, I tried to outrun him, hoping he would think I was just a villager. But eventually he recognized me to be from Mayblea, so I disposed of him," the sailor explained. Karielle was still confused.

"They weren't from Prancera?" Karielle asked. She had to be sure.

"We ain't sure, but they'd not look one bit like they'd suppose to," one sailor answered her, his lack of proper English and grammar skills obvious.

"What do you think, Princess?" another asked Karielle.

Finally, after contemplating this for a moment, Karielle answered him. "Tomorrow, you and I will go out again to look at these people. We'll take Daniel along with us. He'll be able to recognize his own people. If they are as you suspected, foreign soldiers, we'll attempt to learn their plans for Prancera."

The sailor with the lack of grammar skills spoke up again. "So, I'd be takin' it that dis is makin' er job more hard."

Karielle nodded. "You couldn't be more correct."

Chapter 11

The next morning dawned from the east. Karielle had already been up for an hour. The morning meal was finished. She gathered up some food and borrowed Andrew's compass. Daniel and the sailor who had been spotted the day before were already waiting for Karielle.

"You got the plan?" Karielle asked. Daniel nodded.

"It's easy. All I have to do is clarify if these people are from Prancera or not. If they aren't, then we have to figure out who they are and what they're doing here," Daniel answered.

The sailor then piped in. "I don't know, Princess. I think it's going to be harder than it sounds."

Karielle nodded. "It will be, unless of course these people are from Prancera. Come on, let's get a move on." And so the trio started towards the woods that were just beyond the beach the *Diamond* had landed on.

The forest air was damp. Deciduous trees lined every step they took. Leaves crackled under their feet.

"It's hard to be perfectly quiet in a place like this," Karielle noted as she stepped over a fallen limb.

"Don't worry. From what I know, this forest should thin quite a bit in about fifteen meters," Daniel assured Karielle. A squirrel chattered above them. Karielle's feet sunk deeper into the ground below her.

"It's getting muddy here. It was yesterday, too. Nothing to worry about, though. The ground will get firmer again soon," the sailor told Karielle. It was true enough. The ground did firm up again. The forest trees thinned. However, the underbrush kept on getting thicker and thicker. Poison ivy started appearing behind the trees. It was completely silent. It almost seemed that one could feel the trees growing all around. Fungus started growing on the tree bark, and the trees started to appear larger and larger.

"Prancera is so mysterious," Karielle whispered to the other two. She had lowered her voice so that it was almost inaudible.

"Sure, it's always been that way. Ever since I can remember, Prancera has been a silent, magical place. Well, not in the cities and such, but in the forests where the only thing surrounding you are trees," Daniel told the princess.

Karielle shuttered. Daniel would know what this place was like, but still, Karielle didn't find the eerie, mystical feeling enjoyable.

Suddenly, they heard a noise. It wasn't loud, but it caused the threesome to halt. As they listened, it came again, and then again. It was a crack. But not just any crack. Karielle knew that sound, but couldn't put her finger on it. The sound was so familiar it was almost laughable, like she should recognize it in a second. It was almost too familiar. As the party slowly moved forward, another sound could be heard. Before each crack, there was a sound resembling fast-moving wind. *Whoosh, crack. Whoosh, crack.*

"Someone's chopping firewood!" the sailor exclaimed as it became clear to him.

Daniel snapped his fingers. "Of course! That's what it is!" Slowly, they began to move closer to the noise. It grew louder and louder. Finally, what seemed like an eternity to Karielle, the person was in view. Each looked intently at the wood chopper.

"This is just an ordinary citizen from Prancera! How could you get so confused?" Daniel whispered, with a slight tone of disgust.

"No," the sailor shook his head.

"What do you mean, no?" Karielle asked.

"Yeah. Why'd you bring us here with such tension just for this?" Daniel's tone was even more disgusted now.

"I meant, no, this isn't what we saw before. I'm sure of it. The people were much different than this. Maybe we haven't come upon them yet, but I'm sure this isn't right," the sailor explained. Daniel and Karielle exchanged hesitant glances. However, before they could move on, they heard yet another sound. Footsteps were approaching, loud and heavy.

"What's this?" Daniel wondered. "The people from Prancera don't walk nearly like that!" It was true. Although it seemed to be a strange observation, there could be no doubt in its correctness. Despite the fact that one might think it impossible for a certain type of people to all walk the same, it was a well-known fact that citizens of Prancera were light on their feet, and not large-bodied. It was not a stereotype, it was fact.

The footsteps came closer. The wood chopper seemed slightly frightened. Out of the brush, almost exactly opposite the threesome, a broad man stepped out. He neither had a soft face, as the people of Mayblea did, nor a strong or kind face, as those from Prancera did. Instead, his face was mean, stern, and angry. There was no doubt where this fellow was from.

"He's from Euriko," Karielle told the others. Her voice showed her hatred and loathing toward the man.

"Whoa, Karielle. You're right, but... do you have to be so bitter about it?" Daniel asked. Throughout his journey with her, he had never once seen her face so dark. Nevertheless, Karielle quickly corrected her mistake.

"I'm sorry. Sometimes the memories catch up with me," Karielle responded. This confused the sailor and Daniel, for neither had dreamed that anything horrid could fill Karielle's heart. Both knew well that Karielle had seen more than her share of murder, and Euriko's constant raids on Mayblea had left the country sprawled and confused at times. Euriko had committed many detestable wrongs against the people of Mayblea.

The sailor remembered one time when warships from Euriko had headed toward Mayblea, but hadn't ventured close enough to be seen. When the morning fishing boats left dock, some of them had to go quite far out for their daily catch. The warships attacked the fishing boats, leaving them as nothing but a floating mass of driftwood and debris. When Mayblea became confused about the disappearing fishing vessels, they sent out battleships disguised as fishing boats. When Mayblea realized what was happening, the ships from Euriko were sunk in a flash. But that didn't matter. What Euriko had done was a horrid thing, done by barbarians.

Maybe it was true that Karielle had a reason to be upset with the enemy, but considering her close relationship with the Higher, not to mention her personality, neither of her companions could have guessed that there was room for anything but sweetness and wonder in her heart.

"Just forget it," Karielle told them when she recognized the fact that they were contemplating her remark.

Turning back to the scene with the Prancera civilian and Euriko man, the threesome watched in horror as the larger of the men picked up the smaller by the neck, and shook him around a bit.

"Now, you listen here," he said. His mean eyes glared into the frightened ones of the small man. "I'm gonna crush your little head. In five days, my people are bringing huge armies from Euriko to destroy Prancera completely. Got it? Today, you're getting off easy. You can give your petty little leaders five days to prepare and shake in their boots. But after that, no more Mister Nice Guy!" the man growled. To Daniel and the sailor's surprise, Karielle stepped out of the bushes where they had been hiding.

"Well, how about you tell your leaders that the heir of Prancera will not allow it to be crushed?" Karielle said curtly. "Now scram!"

"Darn fools!" the large man muttered under his breath. When he was out of sight, Karielle looked at the man, who was staring at her through confused eyes.

"Who... who are you?" he struggled to say. His eyebrows had risen far beyond their normal extent. He blinked his eyelashes several times.

Daniel and the sailor stepped out of the bush. As they brushed off their pants, the young man shifted his gaze from Karielle to the other two.

"Prince Daniel?! What… you are supposed to be dead! Well, I mean… that's what they say. Sir, I mean. I mean, everyone thought… I mean, like, after the ship went down, an' stuff. Well, like…uh, you know what I mean, sir…" The man rambled on and on.

Karielle giggled. Watching this man ramble on about Daniel, whom she had trained and helped, was humorous. She had never considered him royalty, though she realized it might have been an oversight. Karielle counted him among her greatest friends. Still, to consider him being put on a pedestal seemed rather comical.

He had a rather handsome chin, and his blue eyes were piercing. He was good-looking, as Cindy had suggested the night she had rescued him.

Finally, after the man had quieted, Daniel responded. "Now, I want you to understand me. Yes, I'm alive. That man will not destroy Prancera, if you do exactly as I say." The man's eyes opened wider than ever as he nodded. Daniel continued, "The only way this can work is if nobody knows about any of this. To make sure, we're going to take you with us, okay?" Daniel explained. The man nodded once again. With nothing else said, all four of them, Daniel, the sailor, the man, and Karielle, all turned around and left.

The journey back to the camp than it had first coming from the camp. Perhaps that was partly because each knew what was ahead, and partly that they did not move as carefully through the forest. Either way, they reached the camp almost before they realized it. They were greeted by the most eccentric, yet most annoying person they knew.

"Karielle, Karielle! Captain! You have returned!" The first mate started toward Karielle at a swift pace.

"Yes, Andrew, I'm here." Despite Karielle's efforts, she couldn't mask her irritation. Andrew's happy, overly-cheerful face suddenly saddened to an overly-gloomy one.

"What? Did I do something wrong?" he asked. Karielle grinned at him, bringing back his joyful smile.

"What happened?" Cindy asked as she stepped up beside Andrew. "What about the weird people?"

Daniel straightened and answered for Karielle. "They were from Euriko. In five days, they are coming back to destroy Prancera. This man is the only one who knows what's happening, so we took him with us."

Cindy blinked several times. "What's going to happen? What should we do?" Nervousness could be detected in her voice.

Karielle made eye contact with her. "Well, it's too late to go for an army of any kind, so we'll improvise. I think I have a plan, but it's not going to be easy. It will require the utmost cooperation from Prancera, so I have to think a bit more. But one thing is certain: we do not let Prancera know about any of this, for if they knew, they would simply become so terrified that they would end up killing themselves." Reaching for her ever-present sword, Karielle drew it and walked away, flipping it around in her hands. Daniel shrugged and Andrew started skipping through the camp.

Chapter 12

The bright morning awoke with a radiantly blazing sun. Despite the fact that it was spring, the day was unpleasantly hot. The sailors had not taken well to Prancera's shifting weather fronts. Karielle had known it as fact, but the experience of it was quite different.

"Daniel, how can you stand this? It never gets this hot in Mayblea!" Karielle stammered. She sat down on the ground by the man who had grown to be one of her best friends.

Daniel laughed heartily, squinting at the sun. "You wouldn't like the summer here then. Trust me. It gets even warmer than this. Heat is one thing you'll have to get used to," Daniel told her. He glanced over and caught her gaze. He held it for a second too long, and Karielle left him in complete and innocent wonder.

As Daniel watched her saunter off, he felt a void in his heart. He enjoyed his time with her more than ever. But he left it, just as she had moments ago.

The present became the past, and the future became the present. Karielle spent most of the morning devising a plan to free Prancera from Euriko. She thought about the problem until she developed a migraine. Still, that pain did not bring her train of thought to a halt.

"How could one possibly gain the entire trust of Prancera, or at least the entire cooperation of Prancera to save it, if they already know that after you free them, you'll take the Prancera throne?" Karielle muttered to herself. "Prancera, Prancera, Prancera!"

It was not an easy question to answer. Karielle also had few assets to work with. One, she had the prince of Prancera, most likely her most important asset. Second, she had her sword and a few men. Third, she had her wit. However, Prancera wouldn't give her credit for her wit right off the bat, if ever. And Prancera wouldn't care about her men either. That left Daniel and her sword.

But if there was one thing Karielle knew, it was that nothing worthwhile came easily. Prancera was worthwhile, so it came as no surprise that it wouldn't be easy.

Once over the course of the day she had left her tent for a walk, but soon returned for refuge from the sun. Cindy had been outside all day, listening to Andrew blabber on about a new fantasy he had recently read. It was a good thing Cindy was a reader, for if she wasn't, Andrew would have had nobody to talk to. Andrew would have had come to Karielle and blabbered on, and she certainly didn't need that. Not today, anyway. Today she needed a plan.

The plan came in a very simple form, impossibility of certainty. It was past noon when it dawned on Karielle that it was impossible for her to be certain about Prancera's response to her. The only thing she could do was try. Try and hope for the best. She could not formulate a plan, so thinking about it any longer would not be productive.

Returning outside for a breath of fresh air, Karielle was once again greeted by the ultraviolet rays from the sun. This was expected, but still a great annoyance.

"Hey, Captain!" a voice started Karielle. Turning toward the sound, she looked down upon Nathan, smiling and appearing more cheery than he was. His face was completely tanned from the sun, and burnt in several spots.

Karielle nodded her head as an acknowledgement to Nathan's greeting. Then, she turned to him and asked, "Hey Nathan, you haven't by any chance seen Daniel lately, have you?"

Nathan cocked his head to the right before answering. "Don't think so. Maybe you should ask Cindy or Andrew," he suggested.

Karielle nodded. She had expected such an answer. Looking around, she started off toward Cindy and Andrew, who were still discussing different books and manuscripts. The ground was burning under the princess' feet. She didn't reach Cindy and Andrew, though, for she then spotted Daniel sitting on a nearby rock, gazing out toward the open waters.

Changing her direction, Karielle looked on to Daniel. He did not see her coming. The encounter they had exchanged that morning still left Karielle a bit uneasy, but she wasn't sure why. They had come to be very good friends, and the princess wasn't sure why his admiring glance made her feel so restless and nervous inside.

Now upon Daniel, Karielle expected him to turn around and recognize her. But he did not. He continued to look out to the seemingly endless sea.

"Deep in thought?" Karielle asked when she finally came to stand beside him. She too now gazed upon the splashing waves.

Daniel did not move an inch. He acted as though he had known she was there the whole time, but had never bothered to turn around. It seemed like he was in a trance, yet still aware of everything in his surroundings.

His answer came after a few moments. "Yeah, kind of."

Karielle's brow furrowed in confusion. "Having regrets?" she asked, hoping she was wrong.

"No, just... just, I don't know," Daniel finally said. He wasn't even sure what he was thinking about. He was simply thinking.

"The heat getting to you?" Karielle asked with a smirk.

Daniel grinned. "Nah." Then, as if it suddenly occurred to him, his head perked up and he turned to Karielle for the first time.

"Something wrong?" Karielle inquired.

Daniel didn't answer. Instead, he made his own inquiry. "Do you have a plan? I mean, for Prancera?"

Karielle shrugged her shoulders. "No, I couldn't come up with anything. It's impossible to be certain of someone else's reaction when you aren't them."

Daniel nodded. "Yeah, I follow you." He once again turned his eyes toward the seas. "Well, other than that, how are things going? What are we going to do for the next four days?"

Karielle didn't answer right away. It wasn't that she didn't know the answer. She even understood that the question held importance. In fact, she wasn't sure why she didn't answer.

"Karielle?" Daniel questioned, once again looking at Karielle.

She met his gaze. "It'll all work out eventually. I guess we'll just have to wait until Euriko comes." Her answer did not directly relate to his question, but he didn't mention it.

"Where's Andrew?" Daniel asked her. "Is he still talking to Cindy?"

Karielle grinned. "Yeah, he is. I'm kind of thankful, though. He can talk to her for hours, and she doesn't mind. It's good, because he can talk to her without annoying me." Karielle glanced back toward the camp where Cindy and Andrew were still in plain sight.

"I don't know how Cindy stands it. I could never listen to Andrew chatter on for so long," Daniel commented. Karielle nodded.

"Well, I'm going over there. They've been out in the sun too long. They're probably burnt through and haven't even noticed."

Karielle left Daniel as he turned back toward the sea. Then, quite abruptly, he saw a picture grow out of the waves. At first, Daniel thought his mind was playing tricks, but soon there was no doubt. The image of a man stood out. It was a shrivelled, gnarled and elderly man. He wore a smile as though some deep secret lay in the depths of his heart. He wore glasses almost a centimetre thick. The lenses were perfectly circular and covered a good portion of his face.

The sight puzzled Daniel, and almost frightened him. In his heart, he knew that Prancera was magical, but this sight was insane. As he watched, a welcome breeze came slowly but surely in the heat of the day. He was still perplexed by the realistic image in the sea. The breeze suddenly grew into a great wind. Daniel turned around, wondering how the wind was affecting the others, but it wasn't. In fact, it looked as though there was no wind there at all. The tents didn't move, and nothing appeared different. Daniel looked back toward the sea. The man was still there.

Then, it hit him. Daniel didn't feel the wind either; he only heard it. This fact became more and more evident as the wind grew louder and louder. But just as suddenly as it started, it stopped, and there was nothing.

Daniel looked around again, wondering if anyone had heard what he had. But nothing appeared strange. Then, a great rumble interrupted Daniel's thoughts. He suddenly turned toward the sea again. The man was still there, but no storm was approaching. The rumble grew louder and louder. It was the sound of a great earthquake, but the ground below Daniel still felt solid. And then, just as suddenly, there was nothing.

Now definitely anxious, Daniel continued to look at the man, whose smile seemed to grow, as though teasing Daniel. And then another sound came to Daniel's ears. It was a crackling, like a great fire. Daniel could smell the smoke, but there clearly was no fire. The fire grew louder and louder. And then, just as with the other noises, there was nothing.

The man in the waters now changed his grin to a look of great reverence. His eyes turned toward the sky. Daniel too turned his eyes upward. A great silence descended. It was a serene, perfect silence, unlike any Daniel had ever known.

Suddenly, the clouds rolled back, and a blinding light appeared in the sky. On the water, it illuminated what was clearly the image of a crown. Daniel, now wondering if this was a message, looked at the waters and noticed something new. The man had disappeared. Only the glistening crown lay upon the sea. And then it, too, was gone. Daniel looked upward. The clouds were regular. The seas were plain. It was as if nothing had ever happened.

And this bewildered Daniel even more.

Chapter 13

It was the day prior to the arrival of the warriors from Euriko. The air hung with anxiety, and from time to time Karielle gazed at the waters, for perhaps the coming soldiers had planned to dock that night and launch the attack first thing in the morning, but no ship was spotted.

The princess was rather confused at Daniel's behaviour, though, for the sea made him feel quite unsettled. Of course, Daniel had not informed Karielle about his strange occurrence with the man in the waters. Whatever the message he was meant to receive, it wasn't for or from the princess. Something inside him told him to let her in on his secret, however, and though that would have its advantages, it would also have its drawbacks. So Daniel pretended that it had never happened. But it had, and Daniel could not forget it.

Cindy was beginning to grow restless. Andrew was talking to some of the sailors, and they had pretty much covered all the known books in their previous discussions. One thing was confusing Cindy, though. Considering it was the day before a great battle, everyone at the campsite appeared quite peaceful. She found this strange. Inside, she had to admit, she was quite nervous. Perhaps this was because she had lost her uncle and didn't want to lose anyone else. She couldn't imagine what would happen if Karielle got hurt. She hadn't known the princess for very long, but she still considered Karielle to be a friend. They hadn't really done much together just the two of them, but that didn't really matter.

Cindy sauntered around the camp the entire morning. There wasn't much to do. The sailors had their swords sharpened, and Karielle said she had a plan if she could get Prancera's cooperation, but that was far from a certainty. The princess hadn't actually told anyone what her plan was, but everyone agreed it had to be a good one.

Cindy changed her direction from aimless walking to walking towards the tent she shared with Karielle. She quickened her step. It was not hot, as it had been before, though it wasn't cool either… it was more of a lukewarm temperature. A soft breeze caressed her face from the east as Cindy entered the tent.

"Oh, hey! What's up?" the princess asked. She smiled warmly. "Something you need?"

Cindy shook her head. "No. Well, not really. I'm getting kind of bored. You wouldn't have anything to read, would you?" she inquired.

Karielle started to shake her head, but then stopped herself. "Well, what are you looking for?"

"Anything with words. Though I'm not fond of dictionaries, if you know what I mean. What do you have?"

Karielle shrugged. "It's kind of a manual, though not really. You might find it strange and boring," Karielle said. She dug through her belongings and pulled out a thick book. "It's the Pirate's Code."

"I'll give it a shot," Cindy told her, surprised Karielle actually had something. With the book, she left the tent as swiftly as she had entered.

Looking around, Cindy wondered where she would read the contents of the book currently in her hands. Making her way to a large rock, Cindy started to make herself comfortable. Slowly opening the book, she smelt the familiar smell that all old books seemed to share. She flipped to the first page of the book. In large, italic letters. it read *The Pirate's Code*. The next page contained a table of contents, and on the third she found the opening passage.

The manuscript started out rather like this:

Rule 1, Part 1

This is written long ago,
For the right of a pirate to show.
To tell the truth and answer questions
To bring out destinations.
Though cursed are you if you read,
Yet do not believe.
But read and believe,
And ye shall be blessed,
And forever may your soul be rest

This shocked Cindy. What a book. Whoever had written it clearly had poetic skills, though they were used in strange ways. She continued to read. It was like a manual for pirates, though speaking in riddles and poems. She remembered Andrew mentioning that Karielle had memorized the entire thing, which she found extremely shocking. The book was at least five hundred pages long, and the whole text was separated into rules and sections. She continued to the second part of the first rule, which told pirates to must believe all they read of the book.

Rule 1, Part 2

The truth is told,
Do not turn thine heart black and cold
Away from this book
In this do look
In times of trouble
And save ye self from sorrow and rumble.
But let the word to the wise
If you read and disobey
Ye wilt be despised.
Aye.

"Aye?" Cindy wondered aloud. What an ending for the awkward poem. Suddenly, Cindy stopped. Was she to be cursed for reading and not believing? She hoped not. Maybe she should believe it. Clearly, it had proven useful to Karielle.

But it was hard to decide to believe something in your head and then transfer it to your heart. Finally, Cindy resolved to trust the information it gave her, which would hopefully be adequate protection from any curse. Still, it seemed strange to believe the flimsy paper could harm her. Maybe it was superstition. Neither Cindy nor Karielle were superstitious. Perhaps the princess used the information, but ignored the curses. Cindy finally settled on this idea, seeing it as the most reasonable.

She continued to read. The booked touched on everything from ships to jewels, mutinies to friendships. But it was interestingly strange, so she continued to read. Some she noted to be true, others she giggled or scoffed at, though always within reason. There was one poem that she particularly raise her eyebrow at:

Rule 16, Part 7

Cursed are the rich
Cursed are the poor
Cursed is the snitch
Cursed is the sore
Cursed are the good
Cursed are the bad
Cursed are those who should
Cursed are the sad
When they live
Who can live?
Ye can.
Ye are always cursed
Ye are always blessed
Don't live worst
Be blessed.

Perhaps this caught Cindy's attention because it contradicted itself. First, it said everyone was cursed, and then it told her to be blessed. Who could think up such a strange thing? She seriously wondered if

Karielle had memorized sections such as this, which made no sense whatsoever. When could this be useful? It wouldn't. It couldn't. How could a strange poem about simultaneous curses and blessings be useful for anything besides outright confusion? It didn't make any sense to Cindy. In fact, she was beginning to wonder why she was reading this at all. But she continued to scan the pages, more or less because she had nothing better to do.

Cindy read from the book for hours upon hours. However, the more she read it, the more she wanted to read it. It was a very strange experience. She had to admit that it did have some sort of appeal, with all the poetic passages and confusing wordings. It made one want to read it, in order to perhaps understand it more as one went on. And so she continued, more and more eager to turn the next page.

And as the pages continued to flip, the sun continued to move westward in the sky. Before long, morning turned to afternoon, and afternoon to evening. Finally, it was an hour before the evening meal, and Cindy glanced up at the sky. Realizing how late it was, she immediately shut the book and returned it to Karielle.

But she promised herself she would read it again.

Chapter 14

The ground was covered in dew, and thick fog blanketed everything, making vision difficult. At the first step outside, the princess felt a shrivelling chill crawl up her back like a thousand spiders. The day was greyer than the hair of a ninety-year-old woman. It was so chilly and unpleasant, it was as though the day knew what awaited it. But it didn't, and nobody could have guessed the traitorous events that would occur within the span of that day. It was but one day in a thousand, but it was a day to be remembered.

There was no greeting between sailors that day. There were no jolly songs or fascinating discussions. From the beginning of the day, the sailors rotated in turns watching the sea intensely. This job was not an easy one, for the fog made spotting miserable. But they stood, motionless for an hour, staring into the horizon.

Karielle also stood at the water's edge, moving her eyes across the sea. This was a morning of anticipation for her too, and she wasn't sure she liked it. Finally, tired of the quiet spookiness, Karielle left her spot and went to join Daniel, who was warming his hands by the fire.

Sitting down on a stump dampened by the dew, she hoped he would say something to break the silence. She had to wait a minute, but he did eventually make sound.

"Karielle," he started, keeping his voice to a whisper. "Have you seen anything yet?"

The shake of her head, followed by a quick "no," answered his question well enough.

"Karielle, it might be a good time to tell us about some of the plans you've been thinking up," he said. Although it was reasonable, she shot him a dirty look. But he continued, "I know you're not certain if you'll get cooperation yet, but it would be good for us to know what's up, so we know what we're supposed to do."

Karielle wouldn't look at him, but stared into the fire. "When I need you to do something you'll be told then. It works better, for you and me," Karielle told him. Inside, she correctly assumed that he thought she was being irrational, but he didn't respond in any way. They sat there for a long while, silence consuming them.

When the cry rang out, loud and clear, it hit the princess head on. "Out there! There's a ship out there!!"

Bolting for the shore, Karielle hastily examined the waters for any sign. Sure to the sailor's word, a small outline of a ship could be seen. And when she saw it, Karielle didn't waste any time.

"It's from Euriko all right. Just look at the direction it's coming from. Now fast! We haven't much time! Clean up the camp. Smyth and Luttenburg, bring the ship around the east bay so it cannot be seen. We don't want them to know we're here! After that's done, all sailors except Daniel creep around Prancera's capital city, surrounding it and walking down its streets as if you belong. When you hear four trumpet blasts, uneven in length, draw your swords and attack any soldier from Euriko you see, but not those from Prancera! Do you understand me?" Karielle's voice rang through the ears of every sailor.

"Aye!" they answered in return, and immediately ran off to do as they were told. The *Diamond* was moved, and the tents packed up and buried, burned, or tossed into the sea. Only a few personal belongings were kept, and they were hidden in the out of sight ship. The ashes were covered with brush, leaves, and sand as soon as the fires were extinguished. Karielle then brushed away and covered any footprints as the sailors headed for the capital city to carry out their orders. All were gone but Daniel, just as Karielle had ordered.

"Ahem… umm, Karielle, what exactly are we going to do?" Daniel asked as he raised his eyebrows.

"We're going to the castle," she answered matter-of-factly.

"Why?" he asked, his eyebrows still high on his forehead.

Karielle looked at him. "You'll find out when we get there."

And so they started off. The castle and capital were next to each other, and their locations had been reported to Karielle by her scouts. The princess found it interesting that both Mayblea and Prancera had their capitals so near to the coast. Coincidence, she figured.

The ground crackled under their feet as Daniel and Karielle trudged through the forest towards Prancera's castle. Glancing over her shoulder, Karielle saw the outline of the ship growing larger and larger.

"How long do you think it will take before they make it to shore?" Daniel asked when he saw where her gaze ended.

"Well, hopefully not for a while. We have to make it to that castle before they do, and all they're going to do is break in through the doors. We have to make it in without anyone knowing it," Karielle told him.

Daniel looked at her. "Look, I know you don't want to tell me what you're up to, but it might not be a good idea to make me just run along and pretend to know what's going on. I could completely ruin everything in your little plan!" he told her. She knew he was right, but didn't want to admit it.

Finally she sighed. Shaking her head, she looked ahead and would not meet his gaze. "Okay, I'll tell you what I know. We're going to sneak inside your castle, and into the throne room. That's where the Euriko king will come to talk to the king of Prancera. He will, because he would rather that the king would break down in fear and surrender than have to completely destroy Prancera. When he is talking to the king, and making him terrified, we will come out of the shadows. Your king will be much more willing to hand everything over to me if he is terrified and thinks he's going die, especially if I tell him I can save him. Does that make any sense?"

"Yeah, it does. But what if something goes wrong? Like, what if someone spots us?" Daniel asked the princess.

She shrugged. "Then something goes wrong. Look, I don't have all the details worked out yet. But it'll work out eventually. It always does."

"You seem very sure," Daniel noted.

"It makes missions such as the present one much easier," Karielle answered. "Trust me."

Daniel simply nodded in response. He wasn't very confident in the princess' plan, though. Nonetheless, he would go along with it, since he didn't have a better one of his own.

They walked through the forest. The mystical feeling of it surprised Karielle. It was as if she could feel the trees growing around her. But finally the branches thinned, and a large castle tower appeared from above the trees. It was tan-coloured, and though it was very different from the castle in Mayblea, it was still quite magnificent. That's when the princess realized the next challenge they would soon face. How were they going to secretly break into the castle? But as Karielle had said before, it would work out. It always seemed to.

But this time, it was not Karielle's wit that got them past an obstacle. It was Daniel's.

When they came upon the castle, Daniel placed his index finger over his mouth to indicate Karielle to be quiet. Sneaking around the castle walls in the shadows, Karielle seriously wondered what they were doing. When they rounded a corner, a small shed came into view. Cautiously Daniel led Karielle over the shadows of the shed. Seeing the door on the south wall of the shed, Daniel bent his arm around the corner and somehow his hand found the doorknob. Turning it, the door opened without so much as a squeak. Silently creeping into the room, Daniel shut the door behind Karielle.

Looking up, she saw long, dark blue tunics with hoods, rakes, and brooms. Giving Karielle a tunic, Daniel also slipped one over his head. The two of them put the hoods over their heads. Daniel took a broom, but motioned for Karielle not to. Soon, in broad daylight, Karielle and Daniel headed toward a back door in the castle.

Although the princess wasn't aware of what she was wearing at first, she soon found out. Women and children alike dressed in long, dark blue tunics and carried brooms and mops. They were castle servants. Such a disguise would get them anywhere in the castle, and hopefully the throne room. Karielle was glad to have Daniel along, for she had no idea where the throne room was.

Slipping into the castle's back door, Karielle found herself in some sort of servant quarters. Bunk beds were neatly lined up along either side of the room. Dark blue tunics hung from many of the bedposts, along with other articles of clothing.

Following Daniel to the door on the far end, Karielle was careful to keep her head down, as Daniel was doing. She didn't want anyone to notice her.

Room after room, hallway after hallway, Karielle wondered when they would reach the throne room. Finally, they reached a staircase, which Daniel directed her to climb. The throne room was on the second floor? This, she thought, was most unusual, but she continued to follow Daniel, who knew his way around quite well. A large picture frame stood on the left side of the hallway they were currently traveling. And then there was another frame, and another. The odd thing about this was that all of the frames were empty; none of them contained portraits or paints of any sort. Karielle was deeply confused, for who would hang a frame and not fill it with a picture? Wasn't the frame made for the picture, not the picture for the frame? That was logic that was within the princess' understanding, but perhaps things were done differently in Prancera.

When Daniel stopped at a plain, wooden door, Karielle became more confused. The throne room would certainly have had a beautiful entryway, and brilliantly decorated doors. This clearly wasn't a throne room, and her suspicions were confirmed when Daniel opened the door.

Inside the room were three large cabinets, each covered with dust. It was a small room with cobwebs hanging from the ceiling. Clearly, this was not a room visited by maids—or anyone for that matter—very often.

Daniel spoke for the first time, but held his voice to a whisper. "Okay, we're here. Slip your tunic off," he said, as he followed his own advice. Although Karielle followed suit, she was quite confused.

"Where are we, and why aren't we heading to the throne room?" she asked, rather frustrated.

"The throne room is the second room in the castle, only after the large entry room, but even servants are watched carefully when they come through the great doors into the royal room," he explained. "So we have to get in a different way,".

Karielle's brow furrowed. "And exactly how are we going to do that?"

Daniel pushed back one of the cabinets and revealed a passageway. "This whole castle is connected by tunnels and passageways. I discovered it before, but never told anybody. We can get pretty much anywhere with these," he told her.

She nodded slowly, thankful that Daniel knew of such a thing. But still she was confused. How would the royals react when they saw her and Daniel crawling through this little tunnel into the throne room? Surely not well. Karielle, however, didn't voice her concerns.

"Are you coming or not?" Daniel asked, already crouched in the passageway.

"Uh, yeah," she answered, getting on her hands and knees.

When she was inside the tunnel, Karielle turned back and grabbed the cabinet from behind, where it surprisingly had a handle, and pulled it back against the opening. With that closed, however, there was no longer any light to trickle into the passageway, and it was darker than midnight. Even midnight had stars, but here there was nothing. Unable to see a thing, she crawled behind Daniel, hoping he had all these tunnels memorized.

The passageway led them left, and then right, then left again, and finally down. Karielle felt helpless and vulnerable, for to her it seemed like aimless crawling through darkness. She had no idea where she was or where she was heading. It wasn't a feeling she fancied.

It seemed like hours to Karielle, and she began to fear that the men from Euriko had already taken Prancera. But she knew that if they had, she would have heard something from outside of the passageway. Shouting or screaming would have been audible. Since there weren't any of those noises, all the princess could do was hope that they made it where they were supposed to be, when they were supposed to be there. So she continued crawling.

Then Daniel came to a halt. He seemed to fumble with some sort of handle. A moment later, Karielle was treated to a welcome sight. Light! It was beautiful. After being "blind" for so long, the light stung her eyes, but the princess didn't care. It was lovely. It was light.

As Karielle climbed out of the passageway, she realized why they couldn't be seen. On either side of the immense room were suits of armour. Between each set of armour there was a two-meter wall sticking out into the room, but compared to the size of the room, the walls were hardly noticeable. Even so, they were quite handy for Daniel and Karielle. In the shadow of the wall, they sneaked out of the passageway, closed it, and managed to stay out of sight.

"That was a good idea," Karielle whispered to Daniel. He nodded in agreement. Peeking his head around the corner, Daniel watched his father and mother converse about one thing or another. Although he had seen this sight on many occasions, they were now under very different circumstances, and it made him feel rather awkward.

Just as Karielle was wondering when those from Euriko would arrive, her question had an answer.

The door to the throne room squeaked open. Daniel breathed with anticipation. Loud stomps interrupted the conversation of the king and queen. Looking up, the queen of Prancera, Daniel's mother, screeched. She raised her arm, and her face turned snow white. Gasping for breath, she steadied herself on a golden post by the throne.

"Who's that?" Daniel asked Karielle, his eyes wide.

The princess growled under her breath. "Gresmor, king of Euriko. Despicable man, I'll tell you."

Daniel shuttered for a moment as he walked past the wall Karielle and Daniel were hiding behind.

Karielle had to admit that his appearance was rather frightening. Gresmor was an evil man, and it showed in his physical features. He was a large, tall individual. His nose was crooked and his eyes red and slanted. He had a large double chin, crooked as well. He wore a dark robe, filled with rips and splotches of mud. He looked like pure evil, and yet he was more evil than he looked.

Tiptoeing forward, Karielle watched the royal couple. Both shaking in fear, it was clear that they felt there throats falling into their stomachs.

Grunting loudly, Gresmor approached the golden throne.

"Wha… wha… what… what do you want?!?" the king stuttered. His teeth were chattering, his knees became locked. The castle was warm, yet he felt frozen.

"I'll make it short," Gresmor started, his voice rumbling like an earthquake. "I have men surrounding your entire nation, the castle, the capital, everything. They are ready to slaughter you and your armies. Trust me, we can. We pirates are much more advanced than you in military matters. You will die and be cursed for an eternity," Gresmor cackled, his voice low and evil.

"No!" Daniel's mother shouted in terror.

Gresmor grinned slyly. "Oh, yes. Yes, indeed. Unless…"

The king of Prancera cut in. "Unless what?" he asked in desperation.

"Unless you agree to surrender, *right now*," His voice was raised to such an extent on the last two words that they echoed throughout the room. Karielle leaned towards Daniel and whispered something in his ear. He nodded.

And so, just as his father opened his mouth to answer, Daniel stepped out of the shadows.

"I should say not!"

Chapter 15

"Daniel!" his mother screamed in shock. His father's mouth was opening and closing foolishly. Gresmor grunted and turned his killer gaze onto the nineteen-year-old.

"The prince, back from the dead are you? The hero of Prancera, so sweet. Well, hear this now. My wits are sharper than yours. My body is stronger than yours. And most importantly, my swordplay can top yours. I am better than you in any and every way, so back off."

"I tend to disagree," Karielle said, as she also stepped out of the shadows. Daniel's mother gasped. His father looked shock and confused.

"Karielle!" Gresmor suddenly swung his head towards her. "I should have known you were behind this. What are you doing here? Trying to steal what I am rightfully capturing?" His voice was shaking with anger.

"She's not stealing it," Daniel cut in. "She's here to take back what was hers from the beginning."

Gresmor turned back to Daniel and took a few steps nearer to him. "So now, here you are. Siding with her, another pirate, and fighting against your own parents to give that idiot girl the throne? The throne that would have been yours? Evil of you, it is! What about your parents? You are willing to deny them for her?" Gresmor accused him. He glanced first at the parents, then back at Karielle, and lowered his voice slightly. "Are you in love with her?"

Karielle gasped, and his parents' eyes grew wide. Daniel cringed at the question. He had never heard it put into those words… but could he deny the feelings he had been trying to deny for some time now? He didn't say anything. Karielle felt rather uncomfortable, but for some reason she wasn't surprised that Daniel didn't deny the accusation.

Instead of replying, Daniel drew his sword. The sound of metal on scabbard was sharp and piercing. He pointed it at Gresmor.

"The only reason my parents took the throne is because they thought the last royal line had died out. But here is Karielle, the only child of Tamilia, the true heir of Prancera. I will not deny her and deny the true royalty of Prancera," Daniel declared.

Daniel's mother grew faint. She turned towards Karielle. "Is it true?" she asked weakly.

Karielle nodded. "Yes, it is," she answered. "It's true. My mother is Tamilia, the true princess of Prancera."

Daniel's father looked more frightened than he had before, which seemed almost impossible. Karielle had to admit that he wasn't in a very favourable position. Here, one was threatening to destroy his kingdom, the other was telling him that he had no claim to it. Karielle wasn't sure what she would do were she in the same unfortunate situation.

Gresmor turned to the king. "It looks like you have three choices now. Keep the command and die by my men, hand it over to me and thereby live, or hand it over to her and die by my men, though we will suffer losses. Surely she and the prince alone cannot slaughter all my men. Think rationally," the wicked pirate told him.

Karielle could see where Gresmor was heading. "Wait a minute. You're not the only one who came with more than yourself. Currently, many of my own men are in the capital, sneaking into position, and waiting for my command."

Gresmor growled. His odds had just dropped considerably. His capture of Prancera was not going the way he had intended it to.

The king of Prancera finally fainted entirely. Suddenly, without Karielle foreseeing it, Gresmor stepped toward the king, who was now lying on the ground. His eyes widening, Daniel felt terror in his heart. He could see what the pirate was going to do. His mother saw it, too. She did not wait for it to happen though. As soon as she saw Gresmor raise his sword, she ran from the room, unable to watch her husband's murder.

The evil pirate raised his sword and stabbed the king in his chest. Blood trickled out of wound. Daniel shivered. Then, his face turned from one of terror to one of rage. Karielle saw this. She grabbed him by the shoulder and whipped him around.

"Are you insane? Don't you know that you can't do that?" Karielle told him, practically shouting.

"Do what? He killed my father, you know!" Daniel started to turn around, and Karielle could see he was shaking with anger.

"You can't kill him out of anger! It won't work. You'll lose your skill and forget everything I taught you. You can't kill anyone out of anger," Karielle responded, almost pleading with him.

"You don't know what you're talking about!" Daniel yelled back, and now fully turned around.

"Yes, I do!" she screamed after him. "I've been doing this a lot longer than you have.

But Daniel didn't care. In a matter of seconds, anger had completely consumed him. He bounded toward Gresmor. Just as he was about to stab him, Gresmor turned around and drew his own sword. Daniel backed up a few steps. Gresmor towered over him. His eyes turned into small red beads as he glared at Daniel.

"You killed my father, and you won't get away with it," Daniel started. Gresmor laughed. Karielle closed her eyes and shook her head. No, this was not right. After all her experience in fencing and swordplay, Karielle knew that this was not the way it was to be done.

Gresmor answered Daniel with a low, terrible voice. "And why not? I've murdered many people, and gotten away with them all. I've had many hot-headed sons try to kill me for revenge, as you are doing now. Trust me, it would go much better for you if you listened to your girlfriend."

"None of that matters," Daniel said, his voice hungry for revenge. "You slaughtered my father, and will die today because of it."

Suddenly Daniel jumped at Gresmor, his sword flying in the air. Karielle shook her head again. What was he doing? Gresmor easily blocked him, causing Daniel to fall backwards on impact. Gresmor then walked up to Daniel and, just as he had with his father, raised his sword to murder him easily.

But it wasn't that easy. Karielle jumped in front of Daniel, and gave him time to roll away. Slowly, Daniel managed to get up, his entire body shaking. When Karielle saw that he was back on his feet, she immediately started fencing with Gresmor, which wasn't difficult for her. Their battle was short, and it ended simply. When Karielle seized the right moment, she immediately gave Gresmor a cut along his right jawbone. Shaken by his new injury, Gresmor dropped his sword and brought his hand up to his face. Gresmor was helpless.

Picking up his sword, the princess added it to her own and pointed them both at Gresmor. Daniel had been watching in disbelief. Karielle now turned to him.

"Daniel," she started. "Hurry. Get a trumpet blown unevenly four times at the top of a castle tower. Then bring the armies from Prancera up. The men from Euriko will end up in the city, attempting to slay our men. Bring the armies from Prancera around the capital, surrounding it. But do not let them go into the city. You are their prince, they will listen to you."

"Yes," Daniel said slowly, now feeling rather ashamed that he had not listened to the princess earlier, but tried to murder Gresmor out of his own rage. But Karielle did not appear to be angry with him, which he was thankful for.

Karielle turned back to Gresmor, while still speaking to Daniel. "Leave now, for you tried to kill him out of revenge. You may not see him die."

Daniel nodded. He understood her reasoning. Though Daniel did not see Gresmor's death, he did hear it. He heard the pirate's cry of agony, his death scream. But Daniel did not feel any emotion. He could not grieve for Gresmor's life, and he could not rejoice for it either. So instead, all he did was what Karielle told him to.

As Karielle had ordered, a trumpet was blasted four times, uneven in length. The first was very long, the second very short, the third a medium short, and the forth was longer than the first.

When those from Mayblea heard the trumpet blasts, they drew their swords. With battle shouts and great cries, the sailors—now made soldiers—ran through the streets of Prancera's capital and sweepingly killed many of the armies from Euriko. As Karielle had predicted, all the armies from Euriko came into the city and attempted a great slaughter.

"Curse you, evil pirates!!" exclaimed one sailor. He kicked open a shop door and, despite the frightened cries of those taking refuge in the building, took a post at the shattered shop window, shooting down many with his bow and arrows. In his head, he counted how many he killed. One, two, three… nine, ten, eleven… nineteen, twenty.

Another sailor climbed up to the top of a church steeple and shot many more from there, being careful with his aim, making sure that he only killed those form Euriko. The others stayed in the streets, causing further Euriko losses with their swords.

In due time, Daniel came around with the troops of Prancera and surrounded the city. Of course, none of them truly understood what was happening, but all listened to their prince, who they were thrilled to see alive. But their prince didn't know what Karielle was planning, either. He had just done as he was told, hoping it would all turn out, praying it would all turn out.

But in the back of his head, Daniel remembered the old man and his strange message.

Chapter 16

Karielle hoped she knew what she was doing. In a matter of minutes, the Prancera king had been murdered, Daniel had almost gotten himself killed, and she had slain Gresmor. The princess didn't particularly enjoy killing, but sometimes, like in Gresmor's case, it had to be done. She could not have let him live just so he could kill the innocent citizens in the capital. That wouldn't do at all.

Karielle raised her sword and pierced the blade through Gresmor's lifeless neck. Blood oozing out of the vane pirate's neck reddened Karielle's sword. His greasy hair was limp and gray. She pushed the blade farther until she cut off the head completely. The sight was not a pleasant one. In fact, it very much disgusted her, but she had seen such a thing before. In fact, throughout the many raids from Euriko on Mayblea, Karielle had done it more than once. It was always a sight that made her shiver. Pushing Gresmor's now detached head with her sword, she watched it slowly roll towards the door for a few meters before stopping.

How was she going to do this?

The battle outside the castle was going well. Euriko had suffered immense losses at the hands of the Mayblea sailors, who were all still alive. A few of them had minor injuries, but there were no fatal wounds. The sailor who was shooting from the shop window was still counting his victims. Thirty-three, thirty-four... thirty-nine, forty.

The armies from Prancera watched from their hiding places around the city in wonder. They had never seen such swordplay as that preformed by the Mayblea sailors. Many of them were considered masters, but could see they would easily fall to those from Mayblea. This terrified some, but others were merely thankful to have them fighting on their side. But everyone was wondering if they would turn on those from Prancera.

Their questions would soon be answered. The doors to the Prancera castle smashed open, and there stood Karielle, with the head of Gresmor on the end of her sword. All ceased their fighting and stared at the princess. She flung the head of the pirate king off her sword and it rolled onto the cobblestone streets. Gasps could be heard from the crowd, which now stared at Karielle. The head rolled in several circles before slowing. Everyone watched it with wide. When it did come to a halt, all eyes turned from it back to Karielle.

In a loud voice, she made her proclamation: "The king of Euriko is dead. None of his followers are welcome here. He assassinated the king of Prancera, who has himself falsely ruled Prancera for many years. Hear ye! Look around, you vane pirates. The large armies of Prancera have surrounded you, and in a moment they will come down and bring you to your graves!"

Karielle could see great fear showing up on the faces of those from Euriko. Daniel then yelled something inaudible, and all those from Prancera rushed through the streets, swinging their weapons like madmen.

Karielle too joined the fight, her talent with fencing making it easy to slide through the streets, leaving bodies behind. But she didn't look back. Karielle could never look back at those that she had just killed, for it made her feel sick inside. The confusion and terror of those from Euriko was a colossal benefit for Karielle and those fighting for the same cause as her. They fled in fright to the coast, trampling each other as they went. Their bodies lined street corners. The stench of the dead grew stronger. This was not enjoyable in the least, but the death of the

Euriko attackers had been necessary. None of them survived to the next sunrise. And as for those from Prancera, they were cheerful to have survived.

"Battle went well, eh Karielle?" Daniel approached the princess, who was currently atop a large green hill that overlooked the capital city.

She nodded slowly, not making eye contact. "Yes, I suppose it did."

"Suppose?" Daniel asked, his brow furrowed with confusion. What did she mean *suppose?*

Karielle looked at Daniel sharply. So sharply, in fact, that Daniel's eyes opened wide and he leaned back slightly. "What's the matter?" he inquired, sincerely wondering.

"A battle is never a pleasant thing," she said, now returning to her normal composure.

Daniel nodded as if he understood, but in reality his head was swimming with questions. Karielle was right. He understood that death was nothing to boast about. But it was strange, for it seemed that Karielle was always trying to make that same point. Was that how she managed to remain talented at fencing, yet still be beautiful and graceful? Could she do that because she couldn't stand the result of her blade? If that was true, why did she continue her swordplay? Daniel didn't understand, but neither did he question her further.

Instead of saying anything in particular, Daniel just turned his gaze towards the city, looking out in the same manner Karielle had been before he joined her. They stood in absolute silence. The only interruption of noise was when a bird occasionally twittered in the distance.

The capital of Prancera was large, holding close to ten thousand people, more than any of the villages in Mayblea. Due to this, the streets were slightly muddier and the air more heavy with odours. Other than those differences, however, the city seemed quite like those of Mayblea. Small shops lined the cobblestone roads. Each day they would open, selling goods. Farmers would come in with their latest crops and bakers would be up long hours before dawn making bread for all who would come to buy it. Everyday life seemed quite similar, which surprised Karielle immensely. Who could have thought that two countries so very far away from each other could be so similar in everyday aspects?

Daniel had grown bored with examining the city. He had seen it many times. Instead, he turned his eyes toward the sky. White clouds puffed around in all directions, contrasting against the bright blue background. Considering the fog the morning had started with, it had turned into a beautiful day. Daniel turned his head to the southern plains that lined the south side of the capital. The plains appeared much greener than they had in a long while. Daniel thought it was, perhaps, because of Karielle's victory. The land of Prancera held some sort of mysterious magic, and when good was done, it was brought forth in the landscape. He turned his eyes back to the castle, where they stopped instantly.

He had forgotten. Perhaps he was a fool because of it. He had forgotten his own mother, who lay weeping inside those walls.

Karielle happened to notice his sudden jump and burst of anxiety. "Is something wrong?"

"I forgot," was all Daniel could manage, his throat growing dry.

"Forgot what?" Karielle asked, raising one eyebrow in confusion.

"Mother," Daniel said, still in disbelief. How could he—how could anyone?—forget about his own mother, who wept in the shadows of death.

Karielle still appeared perplexed for a moment, but then remembered. "Hey, don't feel bad. I forgot, too," the princess told Daniel. It didn't make him feel any better. After all, who could expect Karielle to remember someone she had seen only briefly, someone she didn't even know? He should have thought of it. After all, she was his mother. Inside, Daniel silently kicked himself for it.

"So are you just going to stand there?" Karielle asked, looking at Daniel as if he was a book written in an unfamiliar language.

97

Realizing Karielle's was right, Daniel bolted away from the princess. He ran across the green hill. Many below turned to stare at him, wondering what he was doing.

Daniel could feel the unpleasant aroma of corpses sneaking into his nose as he ran though the streets of the capital. Flies had taken over the place, covering the dead bodies. Some birds had also come, some feasting on the enemies' eyeballs. Daniel cringed when he saw this, but he did not let it slow him down. He had left his mother alone for far too long already, and he wasn't going to make one mistake two.

Approaching the castle, Daniel finally slowed his speed. He wasn't exactly sure where his mother would be, but he could only assume she would be in her private quarters.

The large doors of the castle were made of heavy wood, and though they had been beautiful when they were first made, weather and battles had worn them down quite a bit.

Daniel reached for the brass handles. The doors groaned loudly as Daniel entered the entryway of the palace. Soldiers that had once lined these walls were nowhere to be seen. The red carpet, like a river of scarlet, flowed through the space, leading to the throne room. Upon reaching the doors to the throne room, Daniel hesitated to enter. But, ignoring any of his contradicting thoughts, he pulled open the doors.

A cold shiver ran up his back. Blood lined the dazzling red carpet, and the body of Gresmor (minus the head) was lifelessly lying on the ground, dead as a doorknob.

Daniel felt a sudden urge to draw his sword and stab Gresmor's corpse over and over again. That's when he remembered what had happened the last time he had attempted to do something to the vane pirate out of anger. He was not going to act upon his anger again.

Once again remembering his purpose for being in the castle, Daniel rushed to the doorway on the east side of the room. He was ever so thankful when the door shut on the throne room. The memories of just a few hours ago were not ones he cared to relive. They were not even memories he cared to have at all.

Now inside a corridor, Daniel saw several doorways on each side of him. Continuing down the hallway, he hoped that his mother would be in her quarters. It would make life ever so much easier for him, and searching the whole castle for a single person would not be an easy task. Before he had been caught in the storm and joined Karielle, Daniel had tried to do such a thing several times. It was similar to finding a needle in a haystack, though this was harder, for if the hay was soft enough, you could lay it all out and walk over it. When you felt a prick and started to bleed, well, you had your needle. But you couldn't walk over a whole palace.

Taking a left turn, he drew near to his final destination. Edging toward a lone door leading to his mother's chambers, Daniel started wondering what he would say. Would she be angry with him? He sincerely hoped not. She would surly be experiencing misery over his father's death, but he hoped his mother wouldn't blame him for the tragedy. If she did, he wasn't sure how he would handle himself. He would surely be heartbroken.

He paused for a moment at the door. He ran his fingers over the handle. Slowly gripping it, he pulled it slowly. The door swung open. Hesitantly, he stepped into the room. Glancing around, his eyes landed on a lone figure staring out an open window. Recognizing his mother, Daniel walked toward her. Halting several meters from where she stood, his mind raced for something to say.

"So it's done then," she said flatly, not bothering to turn and look at him. He winced at her lack of emotion.

"Yeah," he responded, wondering what she would say next.

"He's dead. You're alive," she responded, still staring out of her window.

"Would you rather it be the other way around?" Daniel inquired.

Surprisingly to Daniel, she shook her head. "No, I wouldn't. Not for a thousand years."

"Why?" asked Daniel, confused. "Why would me survive than dad?"

Finally, his mother turned to face him. Again, Daniel was shocked, for his mother did not appear to have shed a single tear. "When I was eighteen," she started, "I married your father because my parents told me to. I hadn't seen him before our wedding night. I never loved your father, but I was the queen because it was my duty, and it was a duty of tradition. It is not a life of pleasure, neither is it one of joy. I love you, because you are my son. I don't want you stuck in the life I had to live. What you're doing now, how you are choosing your own way, and helping this young lady, to get what is hers... it is not traditional to help a pirate princess. You know that as much as I do. But one thing is sure, tradition is made to be broken."

Daniel's brow furrowed. He took two more steps toward his mother. "Do you truly believe that, that tradition is made to be broken?"

His mother nodded. "I always have, but I've never had the courage to stand up."

Daniel smiled. "You're talking like I'm a hero or something, but that's not really true. I didn't choose for this to happen, or for me to do what I'm doing now. I didn't choose for my ship to sink, and I didn't choose to be picked up by Karielle."

"But you followed her when you were," she responded.

"Perhaps, but it was the right thing to do. I knew that," Daniel told his mother. She nodded.

"So are all the terrible evils gone? Were they killed?" she asked, once again turning to the window.

"Yes, they are all dead. I wouldn't advise you to take a stroll through the town streets today. You might meet with some rather displeasing sights."

His mother paused. "Today will go down as one of the biggest days in Prancera history."

"You're probably right," he replied. "I hadn't actually thought of that before."

Now it was his mother's turn to smile. "There are a lot of things that have probably slipped your mind."

Daniel was confused. "Such as...?"

His mother's grin widened. "You'll figure out sooner or later."

Daniel eyed his mother suspiciously. "I'd rather it be sooner."

"Of course you would," his mother said.

Suddenly, Daniel turned at the sound of the door opening. Emerging from the doorway, Daniel and his mother saw a small, old man. Dressed as a castle guard, Daniel sincerely wondered what he was doing. All the castle guards had either fled or helped defeat those from

Euriko. What was going on? Then, like a flash of lightning, it struck Daniel. The old man was exactly like the man he had seen in his vision in the sea.

He was a shrivelled, gnarled man. He smiled as if he knew exactly what Daniel was thinking. He wore glasses almost a centimetre thick. The lenses were perfectly circular, and covered a good portion of his face.

"Sir Fredrick," his mother greeted the guard. "How are you doing?"

The guard winked at Daniel. "I'm fine. Everything is slowly getting settled down outside."

Daniel's mother smiled. "Good. And I believe you already are aware that this is Daniel, the son of mine everyone had thought dead." Then turning to Daniel, she added, "I don't believe you are familiar with one of our new castle guards. This is Sir Fredrick."

Daniel's brow furrowed. The old man winked at him again. "Fredrick to one, but not the next," he said.

Then, as quickly as he had come, he left. Short as it was, it was a meeting that Daniel would not soon forget.

Chapter 17

Karielle looked upon her sailors, who were rejoicing over the victorious battle. She smiled inside. The joy of the young men was also a joy to her. Battle wasn't her favourite pastime, but now it was finished and the victory celebration had begun. Laughing over a large dinner of turkey, the sailors congratulated themselves on a day well spent. Karielle felt the pleasantness as she stayed back in the shadows of the room, observing the activity around the lively dinner feast.

The sun was starting to set on the western horizon, and Karielle was starting to wonder about this land. For the last few days that she and the men had been camped out on Prancera's shores, no sunset had seemed so glorious. Normally, Karielle would have simply told herself that she was in a better mood, but today she felt there was something else. She remembered walking through the forest and feeling the trees grow. She remembered the day's start, and how the fog had cleared after the battle was finished. How was she to know what it all meant? Perhaps Daniel would know.

Daniel. Karielle sighed loudly. What would she do about him? Did he really love her? Did she love him? She had to admit that she was drawn to him and held a great deal of respect and admiration for him.

As for the rest, she would rather not get into that too deeply at the moment. There were other things to worry about.

"To Karielle, the greatest captain of all time," the sailors praised, making a toast to the princess, unaware that she was in the shadows of the room. She smiled to herself. She wasn't sure if she was deserving of such high praise. She surely didn't count herself among Mayblea's finest. She was still young with much to learn.

"It was a brilliant operation!" one sailor declared, a declaration that was followed by many agreements. Karielle grinned and slowly shook her head. It was brilliant how it had all turned out, especially considering the many uncertainties she'd had before the battle even started.

The door to the room suddenly burst open and a new figure emerged. Karielle turned around to see Daniel shut the door behind him. Many of the sailors were already greeting him and offering him a glass of wine. Gladly taking a seat among the cheerful men, he soon joined in the conversation.

"Worked like a charm," one started.

Another one laughed and chimed in. "Totally! I've never seen—" He broke off, taking a gulp of red wine. "—so many Reeks run at once!" Ah yes, Reeks, the nickname Karielle had heard many people use for Euriko men and women.

"I bet half of them killed themselves, running in terror like that."

"Yeah, and took three or four more Reeks down with him!" one added. Laughter covered the table once again, and the sound of clinking wine glasses filled the room.

"Well," one boasted from his spot, "I brought down more than fifty Reeks with my bow!"

"Yeah, but you were using most of my arrows!" another sailor added with a chuckle.

"We really showed 'em a thing or two, that's for sure!" came another voice. Agreement circled around the table.

"I'll never forget their faces when the captain threw that dirty king Gresmor's head down onto the street!" a sailor that Karielle recognized to be Luttenberg told the rest.

Then, a voice the princess captain knew to be Daniel's spoke in a hushed whisper. "And I'll never forget how pretty Karielle looked when she told 'em all to get out or suffer the consequences."

This statement brought more laughter and agreement, along with numerous wine glasses clicking together. Karielle rolled her eyes. What would he have said had he known that she was there?

"Well, I don't know about you, Daniel," Andrew responded to his comment, "but I won't allow you to say such things. She's my cousin." His voice seemed stern. The princess silently applauded her first mate. Unfortunately for her, he continued. "Unless, of course, you know a full-blooded chaplain." Laughter rose again. With much irritation, Karielle silently went over to the window of the room, which was open already, and snuck out without being noticed. She was extremely thankful that the room was not a few floors off the ground.

A soft breeze met her face as she slipped out. The sunset was beautiful, but Karielle didn't bother to observe it. She slowly sauntered through an empty pasture.

Why is it bothering you so much? Karielle asked herself. *Why should you care how much they think of you, if they admire you?* But Karielle knew exactly why. Daniel had affections for her, something she wasn't sure how to face yet. It was entirely too true that along the journey she had found herself staring at him many times, but that didn't mean anything. *When did Daniel start talking of it so freely, and when did Andrew become such a smart mouth?* That wasn't the Andrew that Karielle knew.

The princess was so consumed in her thoughts that she didn't notice a trio of figures approaching her. She became slightly enraged at her confused thoughts, and the trio came closer. They were three men, each dressed in traveling clothes. One held a long walking stick and large pouch of water around his waist. The three men strode along in silence, and the sound of their footsteps was barely audible. Each looked on at the princess.

Meanwhile, Karielle, oblivious to them, kept walking. Eventually, she stopped by an isolated tree in full blossom. Exhausted, she slid down the tree's trunk, which was slightly crooked. Now cross-legged in the shelter of the tree, Karielle looked on toward the sunset when she saw the three men, who were almost upon her. She wasn't sure whether to be frightened or confused, or perhaps both. But the one... his face she remembered. He was a small, old man. He was shrivelled and gnarled. He wore glasses almost a centimetre thick. The lenses were perfectly circular and covered a good portion of his face.

"Greetings," that man called to her. Karielle did not respond, but kept her position under the tree. She did not even bother to stand up to greet them when they stopped in front of her. She kept thinking, *Who is that man? I know him. I know I do from somewhere.*

"Who are you?" she asked, though not rudely or bitterly.

He smiled gently and answered. "We are messengers from the Higher."

Karielle thought for a moment. She had heard of the Higher, though not on an everyday basis. The Higher was a being who made and created everything, and made everything work out for the good of things. The Higher often sacrificed himself for the human beings down below. Karielle believed in this being, but did not know anything about the Higher. That was customary to most. She had never heard of him sending messengers.

"What does the Higher say?" Karielle started cautiously.

The familiar man spoke again. "You shall become a great leader. You shall lead many nations and become the greatest figure in the history of many nations."

Karielle paused and took this in. Laughter could be heard from behind her from the room where the sailors were dining.

"Within a year," the man continued. Karielle's eyes flashed open. So much good was to happen to her within a year? It seemed impossible, but the Higher, whoever he really was, would know. The Higher corresponded all things on heaven and earth. And with that, the three men walked away, fading into the sunset.

Professor Maddson! the princess remembered. That's who that man was. He looked exactly like her old geography professor. There was no mistaking it. But now, Karielle sincerely wondered exactly who the mystery professor was.

Chapter 18

The evening air was cool and damp. The young boy sat upon a tree limb where, from a distance, he had observed most of the day's events. As the last bit of the sun disappeared under the horizon, Nathan Nelson began to wonder what he should do next. The battle was over, the victory won. He smiled triumphantly. His captain had won. Nathan couldn't wait to get back to Mayblea and tell all of his friends about the amazing happenings he had witnessed. His sister hadn't been brave enough to watch, though; she had run away to a nearby building where she could hide until it was over. But he, Nathan, had watched every gory detail of it. And oh, how proud he was of himself for it.

Something sounded behind him. It was a quiet sound, and at first Nathan was sure that it had just been the bushes rustling in the cool evening breeze. But slowly it grew louder, and Nathan soon recognized it for what it was, muffled footsteps. A sudden chill ran up his back, like a strain of poison was pumping through his blood, killing him slowly from the inside out.

Hopping off the tree limb, Nathan's curiosity and fright led him to walk toward the sound. Brushing back some of the bushes, Nathan continued slowly. He grew confused as he heard voices, for he could swear that one of them was Cindy's. What was she doing? Cindy wasn't be brave enough to venture into the dark alone. Even more confusing, though, was the voice that accompanied it.

As he grew nearer to the sound, the voices grew louder, but he still couldn't make out the words. But he could tell that Cindy was scared— very scared. Too scared. Nathan didn't like it one bit.

Brushing back yet another prickly bush, Nathan heard something even more terrible. He heard his sister scream in agony. His eyes wide, Nathan now started to run toward the sounds. He could hear the male voice laughing evilly, followed by heavy footsteps. Nathan was only seconds late to see the man, for as he brushed back one more bush, he saw his sister.

Lying on the ground, Cindy was coughing up blood. A large knife was stuck out of her side. Nathan was frozen, staring in horror and fear. The once-calming evening breeze was now like an icy hand gripping his throat and choking him to death. Here was his sister, dying. She choked up more blood. Death sweat lay on her forehead, and her hair looked ragged. She opened her mouth to say something, but another bubble of blood blocked the word. Nathan gazed intently at the knife in his sister. This knife was a devil weapon, the tool of a murderer.

"N—N—Nath...an," Cindy managed to say, her voice pierced with pain. Then, as if a switch had been flicked, Nathan bolted through the bushes, tears forming in his eyes. He tried with all his might to deny them, but they would not leave. Trickling down his face, Nathan's tears tasted salty when they made their way to his mouth. But all he could see, all he could feel, was that devil weapon, the knife of horror. A sharp twig from a large tree scratched his face, but Nathan couldn't feel it. He continued to dash through the large forest as the wind seemed to chase him. Nathan's foot got snagged on a rotting log, and he tripped over it, landing face first, but he didn't feel that, either. He got on his feet again and continued running aimlessly through the forest, unsure where he was going, but not in his mind enough to bother thinking of it.

The young boy was still without feeling when he ran into a lone figure. He attempted to get onto his feet again, but for the first time his eyes were focused correctly. Perhaps it was the bright white cloak that the old, straggly man was dressed in. Standing up, Nathan stared with wide eyes at the old man.

He was a shrivelled, gnarled man who carried a colossal book. He smiled. He wore glasses almost a centimetre thick. The lenses were perfectly circular, and covered a good portion of his face. His white cloak glowed.

"Wh... Who are you?" Nathan asked, stepping back in fear. The old man smiled.

"Now, don't be worried, my child. I was not the one who harmed your sister." The old man looked Nathan in the eye.

"Do you know him?"

The old man shook his head. "Not personally."

Nathan's face marred confusion between his tears. His voice rose with anger. "Then how do you know?"

The man straightened his glasses. "I know many things, but only what He tells me," the old man told Nathan, whose tears started once again. The old man's face turned sympathetic. "Now, now. Don't worry. Your sister will live. Karielle is already looking for her. Go to her, and show here the place where your sister lays."

Nathan sniffed. He turned around, wondering where Karielle was. When he looked back the old man was gone, faded into midair. Nathan gasped in shock. He whirled again, and brushed back some prickly bushes.

"Cindy! Nathan!" Nathan immediately recognized the voice of the princess. He rushed towards the sound of her clear, smooth voice. It sounded too pleasant for such an awful night. Karielle was not yet aware of the unfortunate event that had befallen his sister.

"Princess! Princess!" Nathan called through the dark trees, his voice desperate. "Where are you, Princess?" He continued running through the dark forest.

"Nathan! What happened to your face?" Karielle asked as she emerged from the dark bushes. She ran her soft fingers across Nathan's large scratch, which was now bleeding slightly.

"No, Princess, there's no time!" Nathan said, his tears still pouring.

Karielle was very confused. "No time? No time for what?"

"Cindy! My sister, she's hurt, awful bad!" Nathan told her between sobs.

Nathan could see Karielle's eyes grow wide with fear and worry. "Where is she? Nathan, quick, you've got to show me," the princess urged, becoming even more anxious.

Nathan took Karielle's hand and led her in a run through the forest, heading in the direction where he thought his sister had been. He could still see that knife, the devil murderer's weapon, sticking out of her side. He could still envision the blood she had been choking up, that had been flowing out of the mouth. And he could still hear the old man's words, promising that she would live. At this moment, Nathan wasn't sure how possible it was, but he wouldn't allow such thoughts in his mind as he guided the princess through the forest. He already had too much doubt.

"Is she alive, Nathan?" The young boy could hear the princess' desperate question, wondering what Nathan had not dared to wonder himself. Was his sister still alive? He did not answer. His silence led Karielle to believe the worst, and she quickened her pace, which was already a run. Inside, she kicked herself for not checking on Cindy sooner.

Tears blinded the princess as Nathan pushed back bushes forcefully, leading them towards Cindy. Once they entered the clearing, Karielle rushed to Cindy, trying to make out her condition.

Still struggling, Cindy lay on the ground, holding onto her last strand of life. She once again choked on her own blood as immense pain shot through her veins. But she could not cry, for she had already cried so much that no more tears would come. Her eyes were blurry, her head felt as if someone was pounding against it with a thousand pound rock.

"What are we gonna do?" Nathan's sorrowful inquiry brought Karielle's transfixed gaze from Cindy to the young boy.

Karielle glanced swiftly from left to right, and then up and down. "I... I don't know. Go get Daniel and Andrew... and some others," the princess told him, tears streaming down her face as she struggled to answer.

Nathan bolted from the scene, doing as the princess had told him. Karielle turned back to Cindy. A large lump grew in her throat. It was a day of victory turned to a day of sorrow. Karielle felt her feet grow stiff as she stared into Cindy's face, her pain and agony more than apparent. Cautiously, the princess walked over to her friend. She knelt down and placed her hand on the knife sticking out of Cindy's side. She lifted it slowly, and felt Cindy's body tense with even more pain as the knife slipped out. New blood gushed out of the cut, and Karielle's tears again momentarily blinded her.

The princess stared into the eyes of Cynthia Nelson, which made her even more depressed. There was little life left, little of anything. Cindy was going to die. Karielle knew it. She had seen many die, and had seen many dead people. It was no secret. The day that she had been victorious against the enemy was also the day that Cindy was going to lose the battle of life.

Karielle shot her glance up at the sky. For a second, she felt great anger towards the Higher. But it only lasted a second, for Karielle knew that the Higher knew exactly what he was doing, and if it hadn't been for him, Cindy wouldn't have been born. At that moment, Karielle had no idea what the being upstairs was cooking, but she knew this: whatever it was, they were going to have to eat it, whether they liked it or not.

Cindy's lips pressed together. She felt herself slipping away. She felt black overtake her. She felt everything that she didn't want to feel. She couldn't see Nathan. After a few minutes, she couldn't see anything. She was falling into the darkness with only a prayer that someone would care enough to pull her out.

Chapter 19

Grave faces surrounded the lone bed in the large room of the castle. Among those present were Karielle, Daniel, Daniel's mother, Nathan, and Andrew. All eyes were focused on one single point: Cynthia Nelson.

The teenage girl had passed out, but still with them. Although they had stopped the bleeding, there was little hope for the friend and sister. Her breathing was shallow and the wound was terribly fatal.

"I'm sorry, Nathan," Daniel whispered to the young boy. He looked him in the eye, holding back his own tears.

"She won't die," Nathan answered, loud enough for everyone else in the room to hear. All eyes turned to him immediately.

Karielle looked at Nathan with extreme concern. "Nathan, I'm sorry, but sometimes these things… they happen. And it won't do any good denying the truth."

"She won't die!" Nathan repeated himself. He was louder and much more defiant. Karielle stepped back, a single tear running down her cheek. This seemed to upset the young boy even more. "I'm telling you, she's gonna be okay!"

Daniel knelt down. "How do you know?" he asked, his voice lowered.

Nathan's eyes appeared angry, which both surprised and appalled Karielle. "The old man, he told me! He said so! Ask him how he knows!" Nathan was practically shouting.

Daniel's mother looked at the boy. "What old man would you be referring to?"

Nathan folded his arms. "It was a really, really old one. He was small and straggly-like. He had white hair and big glasses that made him look weird," Nathan told the queen matter-of-factly.

Daniel's head popped up, as did Karielle's. Both had had an occurrence in the recent past with a shrivelled, gnarled man who wore glasses almost a centimetre thick with lenses that were perfectly circular, and covered a good portion of his face. Of course, they hadn't told each other about it, so neither had any idea what the other knew.

"The glasses he wore," Karielle started, "were they perfectly circle?" Nathan nodded.

"And were they almost a centimetre thick?" Daniel continued. Again Nathan nodded.

The queen looked from her son to Karielle. "What is it you're thinking?"

Karielle looked at Daniel, and Daniel looked at Karielle. Finally Daniel spoke. "Perhaps the same thing, but maybe not."

"You know that there's a man like that, don't you?" Nathan looked desperately into Karielle's eyes.

She sighed. "I don't know. It's all so fresh. Perhaps we should just think about it for a few days."

Nathan stomped his foot. "But I want to know now!"

Karielle shook her head. "Now, Nathan, don't be immature. We're all a bit frenzied about this. Let's just let it go for now," she told him. She could tell he was still upset, but he didn't push it any further, so the princess didn't pursue the matter. All eyes turned back to the unconscious teenager, holding on to little more than a strand of life. As it had been before, the room fell silent. Nobody said anything, for there was little else to say. The matter of the old man had been dropped at the princess' suggestion and the only thing left was to see whether the young lady would live or slip away from this world into the next.

The silence felt empty and depressing. The only sound was Cindy's breathing, and considering the shallowness of it, that sound was far from comforting. The queen sighed and lowered her head. She walked over to the door of the room and slowly exited it. Daniel glanced over at the door and watched his mother disappear. He returned his eyes to Cindy.

Karielle wondered what the queen was thinking. How had this whole affair with Cindy affected her? The more the princess thought about it, the more curious she became. She became so confused, in fact, that she too left the room to see what the queen was doing and thinking.

Shutting the door softly behind her, she looked down the castle corridor. One guard was at the end of the hallway. Very few guards had been in the castle since the events of the day before, but a few had returned to their duties. Slowly and quietly, she walked over to the guard.

"Excuse me," she whispered to the guard. "Where did the queen head off to?"

"Probably her quarters," the guard answered.

Karielle pressed her lips together before making an inquiry. "Can you take me there?"

He nodded. "Follow me." He slowly opened the door at the end of the hallway to reveal another hallway. He opened the door to the left, which opened to yet another corridor. Karielle and the guard slowly strode through the hall. It was lined with large vases filled with brightly coloured flowers. A lovely, sweet aroma filled the air. The guard opened the last door in the hallway, and held it open for the princess. He did not follow her into the room, but simply closed the door behind her.

Karielle assumed that these were the queen's quarters. She looked around the room. The walls were painted a light purple, representing royalty. Dark purple curtains were hung from the windows.

"Karielle?" The queen's voice slightly startled Karielle. She turned to see the queen emerge from behind a wall. She appeared confused.

"I'm sorry if you don't want me here," Karielle responded to the queen. She sincerely hoped that she was not intruding.

The queen shook her head. "No, I didn't mean it like that."

Karielle stepped up to the queen. "I was just wondering... it must be kind of strange for you."

Confusion returned to the queen's face. "What must be strange for me?"

Karielle met the queen's eyes. "Well, everything's been so different. First evil pirates try to take over, and then we come in and kill them. Now we're all upset over Cindy's injury, and you haven't seen her before late last night."

The queen shrugged her shoulders and sat down by a table in the corner of the room. "It has been strange, and untraditional. But as I told Daniel, tradition is made to be broken. And no, I didn't know Cindy, but she is a person at the brink of losing her life."

Karielle joined the queen. "I suppose that makes sense. You actually remind me of my own mother. Always caring about others, and never being ignorant."

The queen met Karielle's eyes. "Your mother would have made a great ruler of Prancera."

Karielle was hesitant. She had avoided any talk of her claim to Prancera's throne with Daniel's mother. Finally, she answered, "Yes, she would have, though Prancera seems to be a strange country."

"What are you referring to?" the queen inquired.

"This whole place feels magical. When you walk through the forest, you can feel it grow, and the sunset was far too glorious last night. There was cool evening breeze until Cindy was harmed, when the wind picked up considerably and grew much colder."

The queen paused. "Only a fool would deny Prancera's magic. But there has not been one wise enough to discover it, or how to use it."

"Has nobody looked into it at all?" Karielle asked, surprised.

The queen's eyes met hers. "Every single monarch has looked into it. However, none have found anything. Even I have searched."

Karielle took this in for a moment. She cocked her head to the right. "How peculiar."

The queen nodded. "I quite agree with you, though there's not much that can be done about it."

Karielle paused before letting out a heavy sigh. "Yes, I suppose you're right."

All was silent for a moment, as both were lost in their own thoughts, which were quite different. A soft breeze blew through the window on the far wall. It caressed the royal purple curtains, which gentling billowed up into the air. The princess could have continued in her thoughts had the queen not interrupted the silence.

"Once I do give you the crown of Prancera, will your mission be finished?" the queen asked quietly. Karielle met her eyes, attempting to read them. She was shocked that the queen was not resisting giving up power.

"No," Karielle answered. "Not quite. You see, before my mother even told me about her origins, I was headed here."

The queen looked confused. "Why?"

"There is a special jewel from Mayblea. It is called the Lydeen. Many years ago, it was stolen by a traitor and hidden in Prancera's treasury," Karielle explained.

The queen's face showed mystification. "Why would he hide it in Prancera?"

The princess shrugged. "Prancera is very far away from Mayblea. Few would even consider taking the trip, even if it was for something important. Plus, those from Prancera have always thought that Mayblea is a fairytale. It would be difficult to find a reason to take a jewel from Prancera without revealing the existence of Mayblea. If Mayblea was mentioned, everyone would consider that person a petty thief full of nonsense."

"Yes, I suppose that makes sense," the queen said, nodding slowly. "But I have disappointing news for you. Our treasury was relocated when my husband took power. He was the only one who was aware of its location. I have no idea where your Lydeen is now."

Karielle was crestfallen. "It's a pity. But I assure you, it won't stop me from finding it."

The queen smiled at her determination. "You do seem to be able to complete a task. You're very stubborn and headstrong." The queen paused a moment and lowered her voice. "Exactly the type of girl my son would be attracted to." The queen winked at Karielle. The princess half-smiled, unsure of how to respond.

"Well, I should probably see how Cindy's doing." Karielle stood up from her chair. She wished to avoid any more awkward moments.

"Perhaps you're right," the queen responded. "I certainly hope she'll be okay."

Karielle nodded. "Nathan seems dead certain she'll live. His will alone may heal her."

The queen grinned. "Yes, you could be right. I hope so, anyway."

Karielle started for the door that led back into the corridor. "Maybe I'll come back later."

The queen agreed. "I would be glad if you did. Feel free to come any time."

The princess nodded slowly as she reached for the doorknob. She knew that she would be back, and probably sooner than later.

Chapter 20

T he sound of rustling papers filled the room. Daniel sighed in frustration. He had been through almost all of his father's records and journals without finding a morsel of information on the castle's treasury. He remembered his father mentioning that it had been moved, but he had no idea where it was now. The young prince grabbed another stack of papers, this one labelled "Palace Employees." *Oh right, this will tell me exactly where all that money is,* Daniel thought sarcastically to himself. But of course, he wasn't interesting in finding an abundance of gold coins, but rather assisting Karielle in her quest for the Lydeen, the beautiful pink jewel.

"Maybe it's useless searching here," Karielle said, leaning against one of the walls in the king's study.

"I wish that he would have told someone! This is going to be difficult without any sort of lead," Daniel replied with frustration.

"Do know anything about where he hid it? Did it take him a few days to move the money, or a few hours?"

Daniel shrugged. "It was less than a day, but I don't see how that's going to change anything."

Karielle took a few steps closer to him. "On the contrary, it makes quite a bit of difference. Would your father be able to move all those jewels off the castle grounds in less than a day? Of course he couldn't. So we've already made progress. We've moved our possible locations from all over the country to just the castle grounds."

Daniel nodded slowly. "Yes, I suppose that's reasonable. But searching the castle grounds isn't going to easy. Surely you can understand that. It could take months to cover the building alone, never mind the grounds and gardens." His eyes met Karielle's. The princess knew he was telling the truth. It was going to take an extensive amount of time. Too long, in Karielle's opinion.

"Well," she started, "I'll need to know more about your father."

Daniel's face was marred in confusion. "My father? Why? He's dead, he can't help us now."

Karielle smiled slightly. "But his traits that you and your mother know can help us locate the treasure he hid," explained Karielle.

Daniel's confusion waned little. "How so?"

Karielle shifted her eyes to the ceiling for a few seconds, thinking through of her choice of words. Finally, she brought her gaze back to Daniel's. "Your father's traits will show us a measure of his thinking, which will narrow the possibilities of the Lydeen's location. For example, would your father chose one, large place that's well-hidden? Or would he put it right in front of our faces—so obvious that we would never think to look there?"

Now understanding, Daniel agreed with the princess. "Yes, that does make sense. My father was a very bold person. He liked everything to be large and expensive. He wasn't very discreet, though."

Karielle thought for a moment. "Then he would be more likely to hide it all in one, large place with many locks and guards. It probably isn't hidden too difficultly, but once we find it, getting in could be a problem."

Daniel grinned crookedly. "Let's take it one problem at a time, shall we? First of all, we have to find it."

"You're right," Karielle decided.

"But..." Daniel started to think the worst. "What if the Lydeen isn't even in there?"

Karielle shot him a glance. "I'm not even considering that right now. You may be right, it may not be there, but first we have to make sure."

The princess headed for the door, a hint of determination and defiance in her step. Daniel set the stack of papers down on his father's large desk and followed her to the door. Exiting the room, Daniel started to wonder where Karielle was off to. She didn't know the palace, and so she wouldn't have a clue where his father had hidden the jewel. He had a few ideas, though. He wondered if he should voice them or not. He wasn't exactly sure why he was so uncertain about telling Karielle where he thought her jewel could be, but perhaps it was the fear that he would be wrong. As he contemplated that for a moment, he realized how ridiculous it really was. How could he know that he was wrong unless he checked? Still, he held back.

"How's Cindy doing?" Daniel asked instead of saying anything about the present situation.

Karielle shrugged. She didn't know any more than Daniel did. "Okay, I guess. She's still weak, and unconscious most of the time. But she'll probably pull through. She's made it this far."

Daniel waited a second before asking a second question. "What about the old man?"

Karielle fixed her gaze ahead, refusing to look at him. "I don't know, and I'd rather not discuss it until I do."

"Fair enough," he replied. Inside, he was wondering exactly what she meant by that. Obviously, she did know something about the man, or had had an encounter with him. But she did not wish to talk about it, so Daniel figured it would be best to let the matter drop. After all, what good could come from arguing?

Continuing down the corridor, the two walked in rather awkward silence. Karielle wondered if she had perhaps been too forward in her statements. Could she have perhaps been slightly gentler about it? Inside, she kicked herself. Why did she always have to be so bold? Daniel, on the other hand, was wondering what to say next. Had he offended her? He certainly hoped not.

Opening a random door in one of the hallways, Karielle stepped inside, followed by Daniel. The princess wasn't sure why she had chosen this room. She hadn't really thought of her purposes at all. She had merely picked a door and headed into it.

An extensive shelf of dusty books and records stood to the left. A small table was on the far side of the room, a large scroll rolled out on it next to a flickering candle. Cautiously, Karielle walked farther into the room. The candle began to glow brighter. The princess stared intently at it. As she moved closer, she began to feel more uneasy about the situation. What was happening? Perhaps she was simply fooling herself with this new ordeal. After all, what could happen? Karielle tried to shake off her discomfort, but it didn't work. And Daniel's next statement, which broke the mystical silence, didn't help at all.

"This room was blocked off years ago," he whispered in shock and fear. The candle still flickered.

"Who would have come this way, and why? And who would be dimwitted enough to leave an unattended candle burning so vigorously?" Karielle turned back to face Daniel. He shook his head in confusion.

"I have no idea," came his hushed answer.

"Why was this room blocked off?" Karielle asked with sincere curiosity.

"Some rumour about a spirit frightened all the servants, and they refused to go near this room at all. My father blocked off the doorway. It wasn't an important room, anyway."

Karielle searched her mind for a reasonable explanation. "Perhaps your mother wanted something from inside, so she reopened it, and somebody carelessly left a candle burning," she suggested, wishing she could believe it. But then, to her utter dismay, a soft sound of blowing air came from behind Karielle, who was facing Daniel. She immediately turned around to see the candle blown out. Darkness consumed the room leaving behind only emptiness and a lonely fear.

"I think we should leave," Daniel whispered, failing to hide his urgency.

Karielle started to turn around, but stopped. "No."

Daniel's eyes shot open in shock and confusion. "Why not?"

Karielle bit her lower lip. "If we go, we'll never know what's going to happen."

"Isn't that a bit... risky?" Daniel asked, his voice still hushed. "We may not want to know what's going to happen."

Karielle looked back at Daniel. "Well, I'll end up killing myself with curiosity if we leave now. This could be something important."

"And dangerous," Daniel muttered under his breath. He looked at Karielle directly. "I'm only concerned for your safety."

Karielle shook her head. "You can leave if you want to. It doesn't matter." But it did matter. Daniel wouldn't leave Karielle like this, not in a situation he perceived to be dangerous.

The blown out candle smoked as if it were still burning. Karielle examined the scroll on the table. Then, to the fear and fright of Karielle, the feather pen, which had been sitting in a jar of ink beside the scroll, raised. It floated ghostly into the air of its own accord. Both Karielle and Daniel felt a shiver run up their backs. It moved toward the scroll in an eerie way. When its end reached the ancient-looking paper, it scratched down words in an unrealistically perfect font:

What you know so perfectly,
Shall lead you through eternity
That of memory and mind
And the secrets to find
Written so neatly in a book
A manual of a crook
Or so considered by
Society's bold and shy
33, 33 doth secret lie

The pen dropped. Daniel, who had come further into the room now and was standing beside Karielle, slowly reached his hand out to it. He picked up as if it were a valuable jewel. He slowly placed it back into the ink, and turned his eyes back to the words on the scroll, which seemed to glow mysteriously.

"What do we know perfectly?" Karielle asked in a whisper.

Daniel paused. "Something we've memorized," he answered quietly. The princess nodded.

"Of memory and mind. Yes, that makes sense," she looked at Daniel, who did not turn his eyes back to her but rather kept them focused on the scroll. Karielle turned her own gaze to the words.

"What is a manual of a crook?" he asked, both curious and confused.

"I've no idea," Karielle answered. "Where would there be a book for criminals? And why? Does it tell them the best way to rob people? What would be the ultimate purpose for that? There wouldn't be any official written work on crime. What if the authorities got their hands on it?"

Daniel glanced back at the strange poem. "And what about the '33, 33?' That doesn't make much sense, either. What does it mean?"

Karielle shook her head. "I wish I knew, but I don't."

Karielle hated such mysteries. They drove her insane. How could one figure out what such a thing meant? And, to the princess' dismay, the mystery was just beginning.

Chapter 21

A single tear of shock and sorrow ran down the princess' face. Daniel stood beside her in stunned silence. Blood streaked the floor of the hallway. It was blood redder than a sunset sky. To Karielle, it marked the death of a dear one, and a sense of hatred.

"How could this happen?" Daniel asked, his voice quiet. Karielle could not answer. Instead, as new tears formed in her eyes, she turned to Daniel and buried her head in his shoulder, sobbing. The blood, so red and precious, belonged to Cynthia Nelson. The evidence left in the hallway and in her bedroom left only one conclusion. During the night, Cindy's attacker had come back. He had stabbed her with a knife, which had been found in the bedroom covered in blood. He had killed her and dragged her body out of the castle. It was too much for Karielle. Cindy had been progressing so well, but now the surety of her death rushed through the palace like a shockwave. When Nathan had heard the news, he had run away, and had not been seen since. The queen, too, felt the hurt of those in the castle. She hadn't contained the few tears that had trickled down her face. It was a day for mourning, and would never be forgotten. Now, as the sun was high in the sky, Karielle wished she knew what to do.

"The guards, the palace walls—how could anybody get in here?" she asked quietly, drawing back her face from Daniel's shoulder.

"I don't know," came his reply, uncertain himself yet still strangely assuring.

Karielle shuttered as she glanced at her friend's blood. "I should have known something would happen. I should have watched her at night."

Daniel shook his head. "And not get any sleep yourself? No, that's ridiculous. You couldn't have foreseen this." Karielle knew he was telling the truth, but didn't what to believe it. She wanted to be able to claim responsibility, so she could smarten up and make sure that nothing so tragic ever happened again. But she knew that, too, was ridiculous. Claiming responsibility would only make her beat herself up more, and nobody could stop tragedy. Unfortunately, tragedy was a sorrowful fact of life, and Karielle didn't like it one bit.

"We should probably find Nathan," Karielle sais, her soft voice filling the hallway. "He can't be in good spirits right now."

Daniel nodded slowly. "But where could he have gone?"

"I really have no idea," Karielle answered. She shrugged her shoulders lightly. "It isn't good for him to be all alone after something like this has happened."

"You're right." His hollow answer was bare. Neither of them moved. The eerie silence of the blood-lined hallway made Karielle bite her lower lip, and hard. Blood oozed out of her mouth. She shivered. Her blood was so new, so red. So much like Cindy's. New tears formed in her eyes at the thought. What was to be done? *Nothing.* The answer flashed through her mind. But something had to change! Cindy was dead, stabbed to death in her sleep, murdered with the devil's weapon, a knife laced with death. Karielle shuttered as a chill ran up her spine. The hallway was warm, but the princess felt cold and depressed. Why shouldn't she? The world seemed to be caving in on her, and she had no escape from it.

Karielle swallowed her tears. She would not cry again today. She looked back at Daniel. "Where should we search first?" She sighed. Her eyes were red, but she wanted to do something.

Daniel stared into her eyes, searching for something. He cast his eyes to the ground, then headed for the door at the far end of the corridor. "Come on, let's go to the forest. He could have gone there. That's where Cindy first was stabbed."

Karielle followed him, though her legs felt weak. Her eyes were heavy. She had slept fairly well that night, though her discovery in the morning had brought exhaustion to her again. Her feet hurt, despite that she had barely gone ten steps. Karielle wondered if Daniel felt any different than her. She couldn't even begin to imagine how Nathan was feeling. He had been pretty beaten up after Cindy's first attack, and the most recent event had probably left him emotionally unstable. The princess quickened her step. Her legs still ached, but she wanted to find the boy as quickly as possible. She hoped Daniel shared her views. She assumed that he did, considering that he matched her pace.

"Do you remember where Cindy was first found?" Karielle asked Daniel paused for a moment, and his brow furrowed with thought.

"Not exactly," he answered. "But I do remember the area. When we get there, things will probably begin to look familiar and we'll know better where to go."

Karielle nodded. "I hope so," she said sincerely. She could only hope that Daniel was right, and that Nathan was there in the clearing. It did seem rather reasonable, but Karielle couldn't be sure. She couldn't be sure of anything. She had thought herself certain that Cindy would recover after she surviving the first few days. Cindy had been murdered. She had thought that everything always turned out in the end, like a living fairytale.

Everyone was in a mess after Cindy's murder. It hadn't turned out all right. On top of that, Karielle was still wondering about the mysterious poem on the scroll. Karielle shook that thought out of her head. She couldn't think of that now, not yet. First she had to focus on finding Nathan, and hoping that he would be all right. It wasn't going to be easy for the boy, but he hadn't lived an easy life. His parents were long dead and Uncle Gregory, his caretaker, had been killed in a fire. Now his only sister had been taken from him.

"Okay, let's head this way," Daniel suggested. He stepped into the forest. Karielle was beside him, hoping that Daniel had a good sense of direction. She had no idea where the clearing of Cindy's first attack was, not that she wanted to revisit those memories, but she'd have to face them. She'd have to go there again, for Nathan's sake. He needed to be found. He needed to be comforted. He shouldn't have been alone. It wasn't right.

The lower tree limbs scratched against Karielle's legs, the underbrush crunching under her feet as she continued to let Daniel guide her. The tree's leaves were green, though they appeared shrivelled. Karielle wondered if this was once again a sign of the unexplainable magic in Prancera that surrounded the air around them. The trees grew thicker, as did the grass and brush below them. The ground felt moist, though not very wet. Daniel and Karielle remained silent, unsure of everything and anything.

"I think you were right. I'm starting to recognize a few things," the princess told Daniel. He glanced back at her for a moment, but didn't respond. Karielle's statement had been true. She was recognizing the landscape. It seemed as if she had seen the trees before, and she had walked the same ground several nights ago. But she would still let Daniel do the leading. She didn't want to get them lost and confused. She had to do what was best for the both of them—and Nathan. He was the real reason they were in the forest anyway.

"Yeah, I recognize this part of the forest as well. But then, I recognize most of this forest. I've been here many times before," Daniel said.

Karielle paused before responding. "I bet you've never been here on such a terrible occasion."

Daniel bit his lower lip. "That's true."

Karielle remained silent. She wondered what he was thinking. Should she have said that? Maybe it would only cause more misery to the already terrible morning. When she was upset, she sometimes had a habit of speaking her mind a little too much. She sighed in frustration. Raising her left hand, she rubbed her eyes and yawned.

Daniel rolled his shoulders. He wasn't exactly sure how far they had to go before reaching the clearing. He wasn't even sure if Nathan was there. However, the clearing was their only lead, so Daniel followed it. Nathan had to be found, and as soon as possible.

126

At last, Daniel stepped into the clearing, followed by Karielle. He let out a heavy sigh as his eyes rested upon the small, weeping figure sitting cross-legged in the middle of the clearing.

Chapter 22

His body shook as tears found their way down his face. His legs felt weak. His eyes hurt. His head ached. He shuttered. He felt freezing cold, but didn't care one bit.

"Nathan," he heard his voice being called gently. He resumed his weeping. He didn't care if anyone was there. He didn't want anyone to be there. He wanted to be alone, and sometimes denial seemed to help.

"Nathan," he heard his voice again, though now through a different, more masculine, voice. He still cried. It didn't matter. They couldn't say anything to bring her back. His sister was gone. Dead. Murdered. And there was nothing he could do. Nothing anybody could do.

"Nathan, look at me," the princess called out once more to the young boy. Finally, he raised his head slightly. His eyes were red. Karielle felt sympathy for Nathan.

"Nathan," Daniel started. He paused, thinking of what he should say next. "You shouldn't be alone right now." Nathan didn't care what should or shouldn't be. He wanted to be alone.

"Nathan," Karielle tried, "you need to come back to the castle now. Staying here won't do any good." The boy didn't respond. He didn't think going back to the castle would do any good, either.

Daniel exchanged glances with Karielle. What could they do? They turned their eyes to Nathan again.

"He said," the boy spoke between sobs. "He said she wouldn't die."

Karielle felt her eyes grow heavy again, and a single tear slipped down her cheek. "Oh Nathan, let's just forget about the strange old man. He hasn't helped us yet."

"Karielle, I know you don't want to..." Daniel sighed heavily. "You don't want to, but this may be a good time to talk about that man, whoever he is."

Karielle slowly nodded. "Okay, maybe your right." Nathan lifted his head a bit more, though tears still ran down his cheeks.

Daniel turned his gaze towards Karielle. "What do you know about this old man?"

"Well," Karielle started, "if he's a shrivelled, gnarled man that wears glasses almost a centimetre thick that have lenses that are perfectly circular and cover a good portion of his face, I used to think I knew a great deal about him."

Nathan glanced at Karielle. "What do you mean?"

Karielle pressed her lips together, searching for the right words. "Well, he was my geography tutor when I grew up."

Daniel's eyes grew wide. "That's so incomprehensible! How'd he get here?"

"I don't know, but clearly he's more than a geography professor. The day of our victory, he came over to me with two others I didn't recognize. They were dressed like travelers. He spoke to me, telling me that he had a message for me that I'd become a great leader of many nations, or something like that. The whole time he was speaking, I knew I recognized him from somewhere. Unfortunately, I didn't realize he was Professor Maddson until after he left."

Daniel nodded. "Well, I saw him in some sort of vision in the sky and water after we first landed here. It was kind of strange. After that, I saw him as a guard in the palace."

Nathan paused, thinking quietly. "And I saw him in the forest, and he told me Cindy would live."

There was an awkward pause. Finally, Karielle sighed. "Okay, so we talked about it. What purpose does it serve? Did it really accomplish anything?"

Daniel slowly shook his head. "No, we only realized what kind of a mystery it was."

"When you guys took Prancera," Nathan said, stuttering, "I thought that everything was going to be okay."

"I thought that, too, Nathan," said Karielle. "But clearly it's not. There's this old man, Cindy, and yesterday Daniel and I had a strange occurrence with a floating pen."

Daniel groaned. "I forgot about that. Way too much is happening. I don't like getting this confused." Karielle responded to his comment with a simple nod.

"We should get back to the castle," the princess responded quietly after a pause.

Daniel met her gaze. "Yes."

"What purpose would that serve?" asked Nathan. He had stopped crying, though he still sniffled lightly.

The princess shrugged. "Probably more of a purpose than staying here would," she commented. Nathan looked doubtful, but didn't argue.

"Come on," Daniel said as he rose to his feet. He wiped off his pants and motioned for the two to follow him out of the clearing. Karielle also rose, then glanced at Nathan. He slowly stood up, though he was rather shaky. He shuffled behind the other two as they exited the forest.

The whole way back to the palace, Karielle kept glancing back at Nathan. What would they do with him? How could such a wound ever heal? It probably wouldn't ever leave, Karielle figured, but the pain would fade after a while. Karielle had never experienced such a tragedy in her life, so she didn't have any idea how to respond or comfort the boy. Her eyes were still gazing on him intently when she saw him raise his arm to wipe a single tear that streaked down his cheek. Karielle turned her eyes away and sighed heavily. She didn't know what to do. The princess had done many things in her life, and each time she'd had a plan, a mischievous idea. However, no military tactics or imagination could help Nathan in his situation. Karielle wished her mother was present. Surely Tamilia would know what to do.

"Maybe I should talk to Daniel's mother," Karielle mumbled to herself. Daniel and Nathan both immediately turned their eyes to her.

"What did you say?" asked Daniel.

"Oh, nothing really. I was talking to myself," Karielle explained. Daniel raised his eyebrows, but didn't voice any concerns he may have had. The princess likely wouldn't have answered anyway.

As they neared the castle, Daniel looked about the grounds. He knew the place so well. Thinking back, he realized that as a child he could never have imagined himself where he was now. He was mourning the death of a young woman and worrying about her little brother. Although nothing had been made official yet, he didn't have the kingdom, having turned it over to the rightful heir who he was hopelessly smitten with. Daniel groaned. He didn't want to think about Karielle right now. There was too much else going on, too much to worry about. He sighed. What would his father say if he was still alive?

"What's going to happen now?" Nathan asked. Daniel turned his head back, but kept walking at a steady pace.

"I suppose," Karielle started, "that we'll just keep on living."

"But what if he comes back?" Nathan protested, referring to Cindy's killer.

The princess paused. She hadn't thought of that, though Nathan had raised a good point. She hadn't even considered the fact that the dangerous killer would return. They had to be protected—all of them. If the murderer had taken Cindy, what would stop him from taking the rest of them?

"I wonder why he took Cindy," Daniel speculated.

"I don't know," Karielle answered. "Perhaps she was just the first one he ran into."

Nathan looked up into Karielle's eyes. "Can we look for her?"

Karielle's face showed her confusion. "Look for Cindy? Why? She's no longer among the living, Nathan. It's a fact you'll have to accept."

"But we didn't find her body!" the boy protested, his eyes begging the princess. Karielle simply shook her head.

"He's right," Daniel said. He looked to Karielle. "We didn't find her body. We have no proof that she's actually dead."

Karielle shook her head once more. "She's dead. It's like a system, a trap that I've seen the pirates of Euriko use many times. Naturally, the killer is from Euriko. Nobody from Prancera or Mayblea would want Cindy dead. What these pirates do is very simple. They kill people, shed blood, and drag them away. They love it when others try to trace the body. It's like a trap, in which they kill you while looking for your friend. If you actually succeed in the plan, they don't care, because all you've got is a dead body."

Daniel opened his eyes wide. "You're kidding."

"No, I've seen them do it many times," Karielle answered.

"But what if you're wrong?" Nathan asked, still pushing his point.

Daniel quieted him. "She's probably not. It makes sense. And getting ourselves killed for a slim possibility would be foolish."

"As far as I'm concerned, there's no possibility," Karielle told them both. The princess turned around and continued heading toward the castle. They were almost upon the magnificent building, causing Karielle to quicken her pace. She was becoming more anxious to talk with Daniel's mother and ask her what was to be done with Nathan, and how to comfort the grieving boy. The princess could only hope the woman had some answers and experience in this, for Karielle certainly did not.

Entering the castle though a large oak door, Karielle let Daniel lead the way back to the hallway lined with Cindy's blood. The princess thought this a rather foolish place to take the boy, considering his recent memories. Nathan broke down and cried heavily. Large tears rolled down his cheeks, and he would not be comforted. Eventually, Karielle left him with Daniel and headed for the queen's quarters. No good would be done watching Nathan cry, and she feared that she too would weep for the lost teenager. But that wouldn't do. That wouldn't do at all.

Chapter 23

The queen was sitting peacefully in her quarters awaiting some sort of activity to visit her. She quietly sipped the tea in front of her and looked up at the door. The events of the past night had been terrible, as the queen was quite aware. She wondered exactly what was going on outside her rooms. But she wouldn't leave to find out. She was too afraid of encountering something she didn't wish to encounter or interrupt something she really shouldn't interrupt. Daniel's mother assumed that she would be filled in when the right time came. Just then, the right time did come.

The princess remembered where the queen's chambers were located. She hesitated at the door, hoping she was not intruding. Who knew what the queen was thinking? Karielle knew that she had been informed of the horrifying incident that had taken place during the night, but she had no information on the queen's current condition. Obviously, she would not be too terribly hurt from Cindy's passing, since she really known the girl. But what would she think of the rest of them? And how would she feel about fact that the killer had been able to enter the castle? A breach of security? Karielle shook her head. The queen was technically still in charge, so she wouldn't mention it, not that it was her fault. The castle had been correctly guarded.

Slowly, Karielle reached for the door handle. She entered the room quietly, hoping that she wasn't being presumptuous. Instead, the queen was more than glad to see the princess step into her rooms.

"Good day, Karielle. Have you come to bring me news of the outside world? What's happening?" the queen inquired. "Won't you sit down?" The queen motioned to the chair across from her own.

"Thank you," the princess said.

"Ginger!" the queen called out. Karielle watched as a young maid came out at her queen's command. "Bring Karielle some tea, please."

The maid nodded obediently. She turned to the princess. "Cream or sugar?"

"Both please. Add a little bit of vanilla to it," Karielle answered. The maid looked slightly confused, but did not argue. It was her job to do as she was told without question.

"Vanilla?" the queen asked after the maid had left to fulfill the orders.

Karielle nodded. "Most definitely. It always seems to make things taste better."

The queen shrugged. "I suppose that does make sense, though I've never heard of it before."

"Anyway," Karielle sat up a little straighter in her chair. "That isn't what I planned to discuss with you."

"What is it you would like to discuss?" the queen asked. Then, quietly, she added, "How are things going outside?"

Karielle paused for a moment before responding. "Things are only as could be expected. Everyone is exhausted and confused. Cindy was a dear friend to us all. It's Nathan that I would like your opinion on."

The queen slowly nodded. "I would imagine he's beside himself with misery."

It was Karielle's turn to nod. "Yes, that's more correct than you'll ever know. But what shall I do with him? I've never dealt with a grieving boy before."

The queen smiled. "I can't say that I've had much practice in such dealings, but I probably know a bit more than you."

Karielle leaned forward. "What do you suggest?"

The queen paused. "Well, I don't know how emotionally healthy it is, but usually grieving people take one of a few paths through their sorrow."

"What are they?" asked the princess.

"Well," the queen started, "some people like to get so busy with something else that they start to forget, or are too preoccupied to think about their lost one. Others like to talk about the death and reminisce about the person. Some clam up and try to run away from the situation. A few people will want to talk about it, but don't really know how. It really depends."

Karielle slowly nodded. "Yeah, I can see what you mean."

The queen sighed heavily. "Right now, it might be best to get Nathan out of the castle for a while. Get him outside and moving on with his life. It'll do him good."

"You're probably right," Karielle agreed.

Both women turned their heads as they heard a door open. Ginger stepped back in with a tray, on which sat two tea cups. The maid walked towards the table. She placed one cup in front of the queen, and the other in front of Karielle.

"Thank you," the princess thanked her with a nod. The maid smiled slightly, but remained silent. She exited the room as quickly as she came, and once again the queen and the princess were alone.

"So how's your vanilla?" the queen asked with a mischievous grin on her face.

"Very good, thank you," the princess said in an overly polite manner. She returned the smile.

"Back to Nathan," the queen said, reverting them to the main topic of the visit.

"Well," the princess said, "remember when I told you about the Lydeen, the special jewel of Mayblea?"

The queen slowly nodded, though she was confused. "What of it?"

"I haven't found it yet. The beginning of my search has obviously delayed because of this."

"You're planning to get Nathan involved with this search?" the queen correctly guessed.

Karielle smiled. "Yes."

The queen paused. "It will probably do you some good as well."

The princess sighed. "Maybe you're right," she said. "This hasn't been easy for anyone."

"I'm sure you're right about that. Death is never an easy thing to deal with, especially when it has happened to somebody that you know and love."

"I'll talk to Daniel about getting Nathan out. He'll probably agree," Karielle said.

The queen smiled teasingly. "He would dare to disagree with you?"

Karielle's returned smile was half-hearted. She wasn't exactly sure how to respond. Was she supposed to laugh or agree? Was it the queen's intention to make her uncomfortable?

A moment of silence consumed the two women. Neither was sure what they should say next, or if the last they had said or done was unwise. Karielle continued to sip her tea. The vanilla tasted sweet as it drained down her throat.

A knock on the door broke the awkward quiet.

The queen cleared her throat. "Come in," she said, her attempt to sound confident having fooled the one outside the door, but not the princess. Karielle looked up to see who had entered the room, expecting to see Daniel or Andrew. Her eyes flew open when she saw who it was. Karielle knew him. Or, at least, she thought she knew him. She was certain that this time she was going to get answers.

On the other side of the table, the eyes that looked behind large, circular centimetre-thick glasses were perfectly calm. He had known the princess was here, and also how she would respond.

"Have you met Sir Fredrick yet?" The queen directed the question at Karielle.

"Perhaps," the princess asked. Her voice was cold and isolating. The queen glanced at her uncertainly. She was unclear why the princess was treating one of her best guards so strangely.

"Is there anything my lady needs?" Sir Fredrick asked.

"No, thank you," the queen answered.

"Excuse me, but I have a certain matter to discuss with this guard outside in the corridor," Karielle told the queen. The queen nodded her approval, though she was curious about what the whole affair was about. She had no idea where Karielle could have possibly encountered her faithful guard, or where Karielle could have found fault with him. The queen considered him to be one of the most loyal people in the whole nation of Prancera. How could the princess have a problem with that?

Outside of the room, Karielle levelled an icy glare at the face of her former professor. He raised his furry gray eyebrows.

"Who are you?" Karielle challenged. She was seething behind her clenched teeth. How dare this man, who she had once trusted, keep his identity from her so long? She was determined to find out exactly who Professor Maddson was. She was stubborn in her ways enough to figure out exactly what he was doing, and why he was patronizing her and her friends. And why, on the face of the earth, was he a guard at the Prancera castle, considered by the queen to be a loyal protector of the palace?

"Well, that really depends," the old man said. He straightened his glasses innocently.

"What do you mean it *depends?* You can't be two people at once. You can have two jobs, but you are still one person," Karielle told him, her face defiant.

The old man paused. "Well, maybe you're not meant to know yet."

Karielle's eye shot open. Who did this man think he was to say such a thing to her? "What are you saying? Why shouldn't I know this? I'm living my life and deserve to know what is going on in it. I only live once, you know!"

The old man's brow furrowed even more. Karielle didn't have the foggiest idea why he was so baffled. She had made her point quite clearly. "Who are you, Princess, to argue with the one who corresponds all things above and below the earth?"

The princess stopped dead. Who was she to argue with the Higher, the one who had originally given her life? Out of wonder, the princess turned her head to the left slightly. When she looked up to the man again, he was not there. He had disappeared. And somehow, this made Karielle feel better than she had in a while. If this man had some sort of relation to the Higher, it was good for him to be around. Karielle could use some divinity in her life, considering how Cindy's death had upset everyone around her so much, including herself. Nathan was a wreck, and she didn't have a clue about Daniel. Yes, it was good for the Higher to show the princess that he actually did know what he was doing in times of great doubt.

The queen stepped out of her rooms. "Is everything all right, Karielle?" she asked, evidencing great concern.

"Yes." Karielle's answer was simple, but it spoke volumes.

"Anything I can do?" the queen questioned, looking deeply into the princess' eyes, wondering how she would respond.

"No, I'm fine. I just wish that life wouldn't always be so complicated."

The queen smiled. "Don't we all," she mused. "Don't we all…"

Chapter 24

aniel could only hope that Karielle's plan would work. She had consulted with his mother first, and the Prancera prince had great confidence in his mother's wisdom. He glanced behind him to see that Karielle and Nathan were following. They were heading down a castle corridor towards a particularly large study. Daniel wasn't exactly sure what Karielle was planning to do there, but he hoped it was for the best. She seemed to know her way around when it came to treasure hunting. The prince was glad, since he wasn't exactly experienced in such things.

Nathan looked at Daniel. He didn't know what Karielle and Daniel were doing, but he didn't especially care. In fact, he had not even bothered to ask. It didn't matter. They weren't resurrecting his sister, and that was all he wanted at the moment. He would cooperate with them, but he didn't care to go any further. He wouldn't end up enthused. They would try to make him, he was sure of it. But he wouldn't go that far. Being enthused with anything or anyone would be tantamount to letting his sister's memory fade into the background. Nathan refused to dishonour Cindy that way.

Karielle looked at the young boy, concerned. He was not well mentally. She had expected that, but it did nothing to halt her anxiety.

She brushed a strand of hair away from her face, her eyes still fixed intently on Nathan. She could only hope that looking for the Lydeen would spark his interest. He had always spoken of wanting to be a sailor. Although that past Nathan was no longer visible, the princess hoped it was still buried under the layers of tears. It was their only hope. It was his only hope, though the young boy didn't seem to know it.

The prince sighed heavily as he stopped in front of an isolated door. It was made of oak, and pictures of books and scrolls were carved into it. The door handle had once sparkled gold, but the shine had dulled with the passing of time. It was a much-used room. Waiting for Karielle and Nathan to catch up, Daniel wondered how the whole situation would end. Things always ended, he knew that. The way things ended, however, could never be unknown until the time came.

"We're here?" Karielle asked, her voice quiet and soft. She was slowly familiarizing herself with the castle, but the place was so large. She had not even entered most of the rooms in it. This study was such a room.

"Yes, this is it," Daniel replied.

"What is it?" Nathan asked bleakly.

"A study," Daniel answered. Nathan didn't bother to show any sign of recognition. This concerned the princess even more. Even a simple flinch would have made her feel better.

Daniel entered first, followed by Karielle and Nathan. The princess looked around the room. There was one large table in the middle, surrounded by large wooden chairs with velvet cushions placed neatly on them. On the walls, three large mirrors hung evenly. A window was positioned on the far wall.

"Well, this is the study," Daniel said. Karielle continued to look around. The studies in Mayblea looked quite different than this one. Karielle finally moved toward a chair. She sat down and made herself comfortable. Daniel and Nathan followed suit.

"Okay, so this is where we discover where to search first," Karielle started.

"Search for what?" Nathan asked without excitement.

"We're searching for the Lydeen. It's a special jewel that was stolen from Mayblea and hidden here," the princess answered.

Nathan paused. Hunting for treasure. It was a tempting target. He had always wanted to do such things, but he couldn't. Treasure could wait for someone else to discover it. He could not—*would not*—focus on anything else. Nobody could make him. His thoughts were his for the choosing.

Karielle waited for somebody else to say something, anything. The awkward silence had completely filled the room.

"Where do you suggest?" Daniel said, finally broke the silence.

"You said your father was bold, but not discreet," Karielle said, remembering Daniel's description of his now deceased father.

Daniel nodded, acknowledging the accuracy of the statement, but he was still rather uncertain. "How will that help us pinpoint a specific spot for the search?"

Karielle shrugged. "Where would be the most obvious place to hide the treasure?"

Nathan paused. He didn't want to have anything to do with this, but still… "The woods," he finally said.

The princess stared at Nathan in surprise. She didn't believe it. Nathan had not only spoken up, but he had also been helpful.

Daniel looked at Karielle. "Although that makes sense, the woods are huge. Do we start wandering around aimlessly, hoping to stumble upon it?"

Karielle stared at Daniel. "Do you have a better idea?"

Daniel was taken aback. "Well, not really."

Karielle stood up. "Then it's settled. Let's head for the woods."

Nathan was slightly confused, but he agreed with Daniel. The woods were colossal. How were they supposed to find a treasure in the midst of the many trees that crowded the forest? Nathan wasn't at all sure about this treasure hunt. It seemed like it would be impossible to find the treasury in such a large place. But then, they weren't even sure if it was in the woods. It was just a guess.

The woods had been visited too often by Karielle. The princess suddenly wondered if it was wise to take the boy back to the place where the most tragic event in his life had taken place, especially when the memories were still fresh and new. However, she knew she couldn't voice her concerns in front of the boy. That would only bring on disaster.

Daniel, too, was thinking the same thing. He was wondering why Karielle hadn't thought of it. He paused for a moment, unable to blame the princess for it since he had only just thought of it himself.

Nathan was lost in his own thoughts. He still wanted to search for Cindy, but Daniel and Karielle were definitely against that action. Andrew, however, might not be. Nathan was surprised that he hadn't thought of it before. But then, he hadn't really seen Andrew for a number of days. He had no idea where the rambunctious first mate was, though he assumed Andrew was still at the castle. Nathan knew one thing about Andrew that nobody else did—not even Cindy. Andrew was in love. Smitten, actually. Smitten with his sister, Cindy.

He had been able to tell by the way he looked at her. He was her brother; he was supposed to know those sorts of things. He had once mentioned the notion of it to Cindy, but she had blushed and told him it was ridiculous. But Nathan knew better. He wondered if Cindy liked Andrew, too. He smiled inside. But then he frowned suddenly. His sister was probably dead, so there would never be any romance between them. However, there was still that *probably*. Nathan hoped that Andrew would help him search for his sister. Being smitten and all, there was a good chance that Andrew would do it.

The trio entered the forest. It was unusually damp and quiet. It was too quiet, eerily quiet. It was the type of quiet Karielle didn't like one bit. It felt like time had stopped.

Daniel glanced at Karielle nervously. "I don't like the feeling I'm getting."

"I'm getting the same feeling," the princess said.

Nathan walked forward. He felt the same thing, but didn't want to admit it.

"Maybe we should go back, Nathan," Daniel told the boy.

Nathan shook his head. "Nope. Come on," Nathan told the other, older two defiantly.

Karielle and Daniel saw that Nathan had made up his mind. They didn't like it though. They followed Nathan into the thick of the trees.

142

Nathan kept walking, trying not to think about the chill that was running up his back. He shivered. Evil was in this forest, he knew it. He couldn't ignore it, but he kept walking. He wasn't at all sure why, but he did.

Karielle and Daniel walked behind the young boy, each trying to think of how they could get Nathan to leave. What could they say? What could they do? Was there even an excuse? They couldn't understand why Nathan wanted to stay in a place where evil was present. But they couldn't think of anything to distract him with, but they weren't about to leave Nathan alone in the woods where danger lurked. Karielle and Daniel quickened their pace, determined to be there when the boy ran into something he shouldn't. They made it to Nathan's side just in time.

When they brushed back the next branch, they saw something they had never expected.

Chapter 25

Andrew sulked in the corner of his room. He couldn't cry. He had cried too much lately. Besides, he wasn't supposed to cry. He had almost reached the age of manhood. He wasn't allowed to cry anymore, so he wouldn't.

He was surprised that Karielle hadn't come to him since Cindy's death. Hadn't she known it would affect him? But he couldn't get mad at anyone. Anger would eat him up, just like sorrow was doing right then. He reached for his canteen of water.

As he drank, he examined himself. He couldn't believe what kind of state he was in. Usually he was carefree and bouncy, but not today. The death of one person—one girl—had completely torn him apart. He had fluffed his way through life without taking anything too seriously. He had liked it that way.

Andrew stood up shakily. He could feel that she was alive, and that she needed his help. He would give it to her. He would give anything to her. He would give anything for her. He approached the door, unsure of where he was heading or how long it would take for him to get there. But that really didn't matter right now. He had to go, so he would. Details would only slow him down.

The castle hallway was consumed by a dreary silence. It made Andrew feel even colder than he had before. The first mate stumbled toward a far door, knowing that it would lead him out of the castle. He would find Cindy if it killed him. And it might. Even so, he wasn't aware when he headed out just how close he would come to losing his life that day. Had he had such knowledge, he might very well have rethought his decision. But seeing how he was unaware of the things to come, he stepped outside.

He followed wherever his feet took him. Thoughts of terror, anger, and sorrow whizzed through his mind. He was an emotional wreck, which was a condition he had never before had to deal with in his life. He soon found himself in the woods, wandering aimlessly. His mind wasn't working properly, but his ears were still picking up sounds. The words just didn't quite seem clear when he heard them. It had been several days since he had heard another voice besides his own. The voice he was now hearing was low and evil. Andrew could have sworn it was the devil haunting him. The speaker was not the devil, though he did have evil motives.

Andrew would probably have kept on walking had he not heard the voice of Cynthia Nelson. Her scream rang in Andrew's ears. Her scream of horror, her scream of fear, her scream of uncertainty, her scream echoed over and over in Andrew's head. Her scream could only mean one thing. She was alive, and she needed help. She needed the help that at this point only Andrew was willing to give, the help Andrew desperately needed to give.

He rushed through the forest to the place where he had thought he had heard the noise, but there was nothing there. He continued running, hoping that he would somehow run into the girl he was willing to die for. She screamed again, and Andrew realized how far away she really was. He bolted through the forest, unaware of anything else around him, including the old, small, straggly man with circular, centimetre-thick glasses who was watching him intently, knowing the outcome of the events to come. The old man looked up to heaven and shook his head slightly. Andrew's fate was about to change considerably in a matter of hours. The old man continued through the woods silently without breaking a twig or crunching a leaf. He would see Andrew and the others again very soon, but he didn't care to witness what was coming next.

Elsewhere, Karielle, Daniel, and Nathan were peering from behind the bushes. Cindy lay on the ground, tied up with rope. She was screaming desperately. Nathan wanted with all his might to run out to her, but Karielle held him back. She knew the ways of Euriko men, the Reeks, all to well. She knew that there was one thing missing from this picture, Cindy's captor.

The princess picked it up fairly quickly. Cindy was now the bait. She, unknowing and desperate, would bring them to her, and then the killer would have them all. There was either a trap or the man would shoot them down with arrows from a nearby tree once they revealed themselves. Karielle guessed it was the latter, since she had examined the clearing several times, and there was no sign of a trap. There were no vines, no placed rocks, and no ropes.

Karielle was certain they could save Cindy, they just had to be smart about it. Two things made a hero, intelligence and courage. Karielle glanced around once again, devising her plan.

Andrew tore through the forest, motivated by Cindy's screams. They grew louder and more frequent as he approached. Andrew ran faster. He had to get there. If he didn't, they would kill her. They would stab her, and she would be gone forever. He knew Karielle thought she was already gone, but now they were given a second chance to save her. That was something Andrew refused to give up. He would not let her down a second time. He didn't care if the first hadn't been his fault, he had still let her down. If he had perhaps done something different, she wouldn't have found herself in such an awful situation. She wouldn't have had to endure such pain. Putting it that way, her hurt was all Andrew's doing, the realization of which made Andrew run faster.

Suddenly, he got to the edge of the clearing, stopping instantly. Seeing her in this condition, he was petrified.

Nathan couldn't understand it. The princess was holding him back, but his sister was right there, ready to be rescued. All they had to do was go into the clearing and help her. Did the princess not want to save his sister? Cindy and Karielle were supposed to be friends! Why did Karielle hesitate?

Daniel didn't move, either. He was watching Karielle intently with the same sparkle in his eye that Nathan had seen when Andrew looked at Cindy. But this made Nathan angry. This was no time for romance. His sister needed saving, and nobody was doing it. Finally, with all his might, Nathan squirmed from Karielle's grasp and ran out into the clearing.

"Nathan! Wait!" the princess called out. But it was too late. Nathan was already starting to kneel by his sister.

Andrew was still standing as a stunned statue when Nathan ran out beside his sister, waking him up in a flash. He, too, was about to leap toward them when he heard that same low, evil voice. Into the edge of the clearing stepped a large Euriko man. He snorted.

"What do we have here? My trap has yielded nothing but a boy. A soon to be dead boy, I should say," he said. Nathan screamed. "But do not worry, my boy. You'll be the second to die. I shall kill the girl first." The boy screamed again. Andrew shuttered. The man at the edge of the clearing drew back his bow to shoot Cindy from a few meters away. Andrew knew only one thing to do.

147

The princess couldn't believe her own eyes. Nathan had done something incredibly foolish. The Euriko man gad stepped into the clearing and almost killed both of them when Andrew had suddenly burst out of nowhere and dove in front, taking Cindy's arrow in his own side. The man stood in shock.

At that moment, Daniel surprised him from the side, killing him.

Karielle still hadn't moved. She couldn't believe it. She swore her eyes were deceiving her. Such a thing could never have happened. Except that, apparently, it could. It had. And that was the worst part. Or maybe it was the best part. Karielle couldn't figure it out. She couldn't figure anything out.

Daniel smiled when he saw Karielle. Her eyes were wide. She was frozen in shock. Daniel had to admit, he hadn't expected this, either. He could understand what and why Andrew had done what he had, risking his life for Cindy. After all, had it been the princess, Daniel would have done the same. Luckily for both of them, it was not Karielle who was lying on the ground in considerable pain. Actually, when Daniel thought about it, the operation had gone rather well. A bit bizarre, perhaps, but it had worked out.

When Andrew had come out of the forest, the man had been so bewildered that he stood frozen, much like Karielle was standing now. That gave Daniel more than enough time to slice his sword through the man's chest. He had also managed to detach a few of the man's limbs. He imagined that this was considered to be absolutely disgusting though Cindy's eyes, who had yet to encounter a battle. She had hidden during the battle to take Prancera.

"Cindy! Cindy!" Nathan yelled at his sister, desperation in his voice.

"It's okay, Nathan. She'll be okay," Daniel told him. He watched Cindy as she started to smile, but the girl passed out.

"I told you she was alive! I knew it!" Nathan said, now to Daniel.

The prince smiled crookedly. "You were right."

Karielle blinked. She was starting to come back. She could already feel the tips of her fingers and toes. The rest of her was still in shock. She had no idea how Daniel had managed to react to the situation so quickly, but despite her confusion she was utterly thankful for the fact that he had. Had Daniel not run the evil man through, they might all be dead now. Karielle could now move her arms and legs, though she still felt stiff. She walked into the clearing.

"So, I guess today's work is over and done," Daniel said with a smile.

"Well, not quite," Karielle replied, a grin now plastered to her face as well.

Daniel raised his eyebrows in confusion. "What do we need to do now? You can't really expect us to look for the jewel after this!"

Karielle laughed. "No, not that, but we do need to carry Cindy and Andrew back to the castle where we can tend to their wounds."

Daniel nodded. "I can't argue there. Here, I'll carry Andrew, since he's probably heavier. You can grab Cindy. I sure hope my mother knows a good doctor. We still need to properly remove the arrow from Andrew's side."

Karielle shrugged her shoulders. "That shouldn't be too difficult," she said. "I've done it to someone before. He's still breathing, but he's knocked out. He should be okay in three or four weeks."

"Hopefully," was all Daniel said. He moved toward the first mate. The princess had been correct. Andrew was still quite alive and breathing, though he was unconscious. Daniel picked him up and glanced at Karielle, who was doing the same with Cindy.

"Come on, Nathan," Karielle called to the boy who was looking at his sister with concern. "She'll be okay, but we need to get back to the castle."

Slowly, they all started moving out of the forest. They left the evil man's remains behind, since he was clearly dead and in more than one piece. Karielle guessed he had deserted the Euriko army out of fear when they arrived. He had seen his comrades killed and wanted to return to his country with honour. That was why he tried to murder them all, using Cindy as bait.

149

The evil feeling that was in the forest when they had entered was now gone and replaced with a bright, pleasant mood. Birds began to twitter in the branches above. The sky was perfectly blue and cloudless. The air smelled fresh and new.

Karielle was glad. The evil feeling before hadn't been one she enjoyed in the least. When they had saved Prancera from Euriko, the princess had hoped that the evil was gone. That had obviously not been true. The devilish pirates, however, were now gone for the time being. The princess was extremely thankful. She needed a few days to rest and clear her head of the unpleasant events. It had had been a troubling few days. She had all the confidence in the world that Cindy and Andrew would recover, though, and of that she was glad.

Chapter 26

The queen silently catered to Cindy's wounds. She smiled at the girl. The queen had not expected her to be alive, and it had been a wonderful surprise to everyone who knew her. Of course, the queen was also thankful for the safety of the rest of the youth, including her son. She couldn't imagine such a violent experience, a scene filled with such depravity. She did not wish to imagine it, though. She had never been one for battles. She fainted easily.

Cindy looked into the face of the regal woman. Her grin didn't reveal what the queen was thinking, and Cindy was slightly disappointed at this. She had been through so much in the last few days, she really wanted to know what people were thinking. What were they thinking about her and about life in general? How had her disappearance affected them? It obviously had affected them, Andrew especially.

The girl groaned. She wasn't sure how she was to approach Andrew yet. Perhaps in a few days she'd be ready, but not right then. She had to sort a few things out first. She had to admit that she had thought about Andrew a lot in her distress, but she wasn't ready to face that reality. Right then, all she wanted to think about was her recovery.

"Mother," Daniel called from across the room. Both women turned their heads. The queen started walking to her son. Andrew, who was still unconscious, lay on a cot before them.

"Is something wrong?" the queen inquired.

Daniel paused and knelt beside the cot. "I got the arrow out," he started. "I've cleaned it and got the bleeding to stop."

"That's great. What do you want to know?" the queen asked.

"What do I do now?" the prince asked, confused.

The queen shrugged her shoulders. "Wait. What else can you do?"

Daniel blinked a few times. "Wait?"

"In a few days, you'll know how he is, but you can't get an accurate idea of his condition right now. I mean, you could guess, but that's not going to do him any good."

"So I'm done. That's it?" Daniel asked.

The queen laughed at her son's remark. "What do you mean, *that's it?* You've been working on him for hours!"

Daniel grinned. "Yeah, I guess. I just presumed that I would be working on him several more hours."

The queen smiled in return. "Medical work may be long and exhausting, but it's not *that* long and exhausting."

"I should probably go find Karielle and inform her of our patient's conditions," Daniel told his mother with a satisfied sigh.

The queen smirked slyly and shot her son a mischievous look. She wasn't sure that giving the princess information was the only reason he wanted to see her. She didn't comment, though.

Daniel headed for the door. He felt tired, but was glad that his work was done for the day. Digging inside the human body wasn't exactly his idea of amusement. It was more like stressful work. He was anxious to get some sleep, but first he needed to report to the princess. He didn't mind making the trip. In fact, he did it half for duty, half for pleasure. It gave him another excuse to see Karielle.

Sauntering down the corridor, Daniel hoped that Karielle was in his mother's quarters. She had been sleeping in there for the last few days. If she wasn't, she was probably with Nathan. If she wasn't with Nathan, Daniel had no idea where she would be. Karielle wasn't one to be tied down easily, and Daniel knew this. He actually liked that about her. She was free and adventurous. And she was beautiful. Daniel hadn't ever met a girl like her before, which was understandable, for the princess was definitely one of a kind.

Daniel headed down another hallway towards his mother's rooms. His legs started dragging. It had been a long day. His mind flashed back to the events that had passed. It was sheer providence that it had all worked out in the end with everyone alive. Andrew and Cindy had both come close to death in the last week. It sincerely shocked Daniel that it had only been a week. It seemed more like a year. When he thought back to the battle against Euriko, it felt like it could have happened an eternity ago. So much had happened since then.

Knocking on the door that was the entrance to his mother's quarters, Daniel prayed that Karielle would answer. She did.

"Come in," the princess said, her words sounding tired.

Daniel stepped into the room. Karielle was sitting by herself at a lone table. He sat down beside her.

"Andrew and Cindy are doing fine," he stated. Karielle didn't acknowledge his words. She stared blankly.

Daniel, now feeling rather awkward in the silence, wondered what he should do next. He looked at Karielle more closely. She did not meet his gaze. Daniel could see she was lost in thought. What was she thinking about? Karielle wasn't usually one to lose herself in thought. Most of the time, she was attentive and alert. Feeling unsure, he contemplated how to get her out of her daze. Should he say something again?

"Karielle," he said, now louder than before. She still did not respond. "Karielle," he repeated with even more volume.

She jumped slightly, looking at Daniel. The stunned look on her face was hardly disguised. "How did you get in here?" she questioned.

Daniel grinned, "Through the door."

The princess looked blankly at him. "Oh."

Daniel's smile grew. "You told me I could come in."

"I did?" Karielle asked.

"Uh, yeah. Just like twenty seconds ago," Daniel told her, his smirk still growing.

Karielle bit her lower lips before responding. "I suppose I must have been dreaming."

Daniel laughed at this. "Yeah, I guess.

"Well," the princess started, fidgeting uncomfortably, "what are you doing here?"

Daniel repeated his message: "Andrew and Cindy are doing fine. I thought you might want to know."

"Oh yes," Karielle quickly replied. "Thanks for telling me. Do you think they'll pull through?"

Daniel nodded. "Definitely," he answered.

"Good." Karielle said. She waited for Daniel to say something else. He didn't. Silence followed. Neither knew what to say next. The princess wondered if he would leave, but, surprisingly enough, he remained at the table. He wondered if she would ask him to leave, or at least ask him on what his intentions were. But she didn't. She was as he was, silent.

Although there was quiet in the room, the minds of the two were far from soundless. While thoughts ran wildly through their minds, they both assumed that the other wasn't feeling as uncomfortable as them. It made a rather odd dynamic they shared.

Eventually, after sitting for far too long, it was the queen who broke the awkward moment. It relieved both to hear the soft knock on the door.

"Come in," Karielle said, this time aware of her words.

The queen complied, slowly opening the door and examining the two in front of her. She was surprised she hadn't heard them talking. She would have assumed them to be divulging in some sort of interesting topic. Daniel began to wish that they had started an appealing conversation. It would have ended the strange silence from consuming the room completely.

Instead of asking the two any questions, the queen simply took a chair and sat at the round table as well, thinking that they would invite her into the conversation they were having. Of course, this didn't happen easily, since Daniel and Karielle weren't exactly having a conversation.

The queen looked nervously from one to the other. "So, our patients are doing well."

Daniel nodded, but remained silent.

"That's good," Karielle answered, simplistically and obviously.

"Yes," the queen agreed.

Daniel looked up toward the sky, wondering if there would be an end to this meeting. Perhaps he should just leave.

"Any other news?" Karielle asked uncertainly.

"Not really," the queen replied.

"I think I might leave you two alone for the rest of the night," Daniel finally said. He got up and headed for the door. He was unsure what his mother and Karielle would talk about after he was gone, or if they would talk at all. When he had been with the princess, he sure hadn't gotten too far. It was strange for Karielle to have been so quiet. But she had certainly been that night. Perhaps she was just tired.

Daniel closed the door behind him.

Chapter 27

Karielle visited Cindy when the sun dawned the next morning. Sitting by her bedside, the princess was both surprised and pleased to know that Cindy was well enough to carry on a decent conversation and stay awake.

"What's been happening while I was... umm... missing?" Cindy asked.

The princess grinned. "We couldn't do much with you gone."

Cindy bit her lip. "Must have been quite the mystery."

"There have been too many mysteries in my life lately. First, Euriko soldiers showed up, then you were stabbed, then there was the incident with the eerie room, and then you went missing, and that strange old man was present through it all."

Cindy looked at the princess curiously. "What eerie room?"

Karielle remembered that Cindy wouldn't have heard about the strange room, for neither she nor Daniel had actually told anyone about it. Quickly grazing through the story of the odd room that had been sealed off, the princess recited the strange poem for her friend.

"Does it make any sense to you?" Karielle inquired. Cindy shrugged. Karielle's eyes widened in amazement. Could Cindy actually be able to translate the poem that neither she nor Daniel had understood in the least?

"Remember when, before the battle…" Cindy trailed off.

"Go on," Karielle said slowly.

"You lent me your book, the Pirate's Code or something like that.

Karielle was confused. "What about it?"

"Well, you've memorized that, which would fit into 'of memory and mind.' It's also been around for a long time, you know 'lead you through eternity.' But, what makes me sure is where it says talks about the 'manual of a crook or so considered by, society's bold and shy.'"

"Sure of what? What does that mean?" The princess leaned in closer to Cindy.

"Well, those from Mayblea aren't crooks. They're not really pirates, either. However, they would have been considered to be crooks by society here before the battle with Euriko. The Pirate's Code is a manual for you, who would be considered a crook. Get it?"

Karielle nodded. "That actually makes sense. It's not even complicated. I suppose the 33, 33 would mean rule 33, part 33 in the book."

"That would be my guess," Cindy replied. "Do you have the book close by? Can you see what that rule says?"

The princess smiled. "I don't need the book. Have you forgotten? I have it all memorized."

Cindy returned the grin. "Right. I momentarily forgot. So what does it say?"

Karielle paused. She could see the page that it was written on.

Rule 33, Part 33

The day of sorrows will come
Despite all enemies that run
Evil will still remain
It will drive until insane
Supposed death will follow
Tears will come on the morrow
But do not despair
For in the end,

157

The courage of a friend,
Will lead all through
The only question is who.
And everything will work out in the end
Just as the Higher commands.

"It's... strangely beautiful," Cindy said after Karielle had recited the passage.

Karielle laughed. "Most poems in this book are. How many did you read when you had it?"

Cindy paused. "A lot. Honestly, I don't even remember. Some of them are really weird, though."

"I can't argue with you there. Some of them don't make any sense whatsoever. I still have them memorized, though."

"Why?" Cindy inquired.

The princess shrugged. "You never know when they might be useful. You'd be surprised how many I've used so far."

"Really?" Cindy was curious.

The princess nodded. "Yes. Many of the ancient poems and phrases can come in handy in today's world. I mean, they cover a lot of topics."

Cindy could only agree with that. "They do cover a lot. I remember reading about everything from curses to oatmeal."

The princess grinned. "There is a poem about oatmeal there. It's pretty short, though. I believe it says

Hear ye! Hear ye! Hear ye!
When you eat oatmeal sloppy don't be.
A good impression will follow
if you correctly eat and swallow
your morning meal."

Cindy giggled. "I always eat my oatmeal properly."

Karielle's smile grew. "I'll have to admit, I've never used that before. But you never know."

158

"Maybe someday you'll make an impression eating breakfast," Cindy told the princess, her giggle still written on her face. Both teenagers laughed once again.

The visit had been more than joyous, it had been comical. Of course, it became even more comical when the queen sent in a maid to invite them all to a proper breakfast the next morning. Cindy and Karielle couldn't help but laugh when the maid told them that this would be a proper meal for etiquette. The maid was more than bewildered, but the two didn't seem to care. They kept on laughing.

Chapter 28

"This is really good oatmeal," Cindy told the queen. The fact that oatmeal was being served came to the Cindy and Karielle as a hysterical surprise. They were still trying to contain their laughter.

The queen smiled pleasantly. "I'm glad you think so. I thought it was time that we all got together to have a proper meal." The queen looked down the breakfast table, decorated with a dark green tablecloth that was accented with lace. She felt pleased. She was at the head of the table. Daniel sat on her right, Karielle on her left. Beside Daniel there was Andrew, who had surprisingly been well enough to join them. Cindy was facing Andrew and next to Karielle. Nathan sat at the end of the table.

"So, what's happening today?" Daniel asked his table companions.

Karielle shrugged. "Well, we may as well keep looking for the jewel. It's not like we've found it yet."

Daniel agreed. "It seems like a reasonable plan."

The queen smiled. "Reasonable, yes, but not needed."

Karielle looked at the queen curiously. "What do you mean? Why don't we need to look for the Lydeen?"

The queen's smile grew. "Last night, before I headed to bed, I accidentally dropped one of my emeralds. It just happened to be one of the large and heavy ones. The sound it made when it hit the floor was peculiar, so I went to investigate. I ended up smashing the plank in my bedroom with a chest full of rocks. You know what had been under my floor the whole time?"

"The treasury!" Nathan exclaimed, his eyes wide. He had been extremely happy to have his sister back, which was more than understandable.

The queen nodded. "All those riches were under my bedroom floor the whole time."

"Was the Lydeen there?" Karielle asked slowly.

The queen shook her head, and Karielle's spirits fell. "However," the queen started again, "I did find your jewel."

"You must have found an awful lot last night. Where was the Lydeen?" Daniel asked his mother.

The queen paused before responding. "We have a historical chest in the castle. It's where you'd find records from ancient kings and old feather pens that scribes used hundreds of years ago. Some castle occupants even stored favourite possessions in it. We have a blanket more than a hundred years old from Prince Albert. He loved it when he was a toddler."

"The jewel was in there?" Karielle inquired.

The queen nodded. "The clue was hidden in Princess Rebecca's diary. After reading the diary, I learned that the maid that had seen the mysterious man put the Lydeen in the treasury, taken it, and passed it along to her mistress. Apparently she had been unsure of what she should do with it. Of course, the princess didn't know either, so she hid it in her diary and wondered if anyone would ask about it. When nobody did, she kept it."

Karielle looked at the queen. "Do you have it with you?" she asked.

Once again, the queen nodded. She pulled out a large, pink jewel from her dress. It sparkled in the daylight.

"It's lovely," the princess said in awe.

"That it is. I was stunned when I first saw it. No wonder it was so special to Mayblea's ancient monarchs. It would be important to me, that's for sure."

Karielle had never suspected the jewel would glisten so brightly or so beautifully. She was thankful it had been found. The princess now understood the great lengths that the ancient king had taken in hiding it, and how Sir Linden's revenge had felt so complete by stealing the jewel so many years ago.

"You know…" Cindy started.

"What?" asked Andrew, looking her in the eye.

"Everything always seems to work out in the end. I mean, look where we were last week. We were all a wreck. Now we're all together, happy and healthy. Well, mostly healthy."

"Healthy, yes. Healed, not quite," Andrew corrected her.

"You're right, Cindy," the princess agreed. "It did all work out beautifully. It looks like we can pretty much move on now. There are no more mysteries to solve, no more worrying to do."

Daniel smiled. "Well, that's not entirely accurate."

"Whatever do you mean?" asked Karielle, her eyes wide.

"The old man is still a mystery. We still don't know who he is or where he comes from," Daniel explained.

Karielle sighed, realizing that he was correct. "We may never know that. Maybe we're not supposed to know."

The queen looked Karielle in the eye. "Oh, I'm sure you'll know it someday. It's just that it's one of those things you can't control. You really can't decide when you'll figure it out. Still, in all likelihood, it will be revealed to you."

"I hope so," Karielle replied.

"I saw the old man a few times when I was kidnapped," Cindy said, more to herself than to anyone else, but everyone perked up instantly.

"What did he say to you?" Andrew asked, his eyes filled with a concern that made Karielle grin.

"He didn't say anything. He simply showed up once and a while. His presence brought me comfort, though."

"Why?" the queen inquired. She still wasn't so sure what everyone meant when they were discussing the old man, but she had come to get some idea of him and why he was making them so upset and curious.

"It made me remember that there was still good out there and that someone was watching out for me," Cindy explained. "I wasn't completely alone with the killer."

The princess nodded. "Of course. It would make sense for you to like the feeling that you hadn't been abandoned. Not that we abandoned you... but you get what I mean."

Cindy smiled. "Yeah."

"How about we forget about this whole ordeal and continue eating our meal," the queen suggested. All eyes turned to her.

"I like your rhyme, mother," Daniel said after a moment of silence.

"What rhyme?" she asked him.

"Ordeal and meal, they rhyme," he responded with a smile and a quick wink. She returned the grin.

"Umm, does anyone have the sugar?" the princess asked nervously. The conversation about the old man ended a little too suddenly.

"Here," Daniel said as he handed her a small bowl full of the tiny white particles. As she took it from him, she could feel his gaze upon her. It wasn't quite a regular gaze, though. Karielle wasn't completely stunned by this, but she was slightly surprised when she realized how much she enjoyed it. She knew she was attracted to Daniel, but she hadn't realized how much.

The morning meal ended quickly enough, and by the time the last morsel of food had been taken away, Cindy and Karielle had completely forgotten about the oatmeal poem. They were too happy reflecting on how everything had come together so nicely.

Karielle brought the Lydeen to the rooms she was sharing with the queen. It still sparkled. As the princess entered the room, she almost ran into the queen, who was waiting there for her.

"Oh, sorry," Karielle apologized quickly. "Is there something you would like?"

The queen paused, wondering how she should start the conversation with the princess. "Want some tea?"

"Sure," Karielle answered uncertainly. What was the queen getting at? Both women moved towards the table and sat down. The princess wondered how many times she had sat down at this table with somebody or other. Taking her seat, the queen motioned for Ginger and instructed her to bring them tea. Vanilla tea, to be exact. Karielle smiled.

"When are you planning on being crowned?" the queen asked.

Karielle's eyes shot open. She hadn't even thought of being crowned. She wasn't sure that she wanted to go through with a ceremony, but it was probably tradition. In Mayblea, a coronation was traditional as well. Karielle didn't respond for a while. Finally, still uncertain of what she was suggesting, she looked directly at the queen. "I don't know," was her all-too-simple response.

The queen grinned. "I suppose you haven't been thinking much about it lately."

"Not at all, actually," Karielle replied.

"You know," the queen started, "it would be really neat if we had the wedding and coronation on the same day, don't you think?"

Karielle raised her left eyebrow. "Wedding? Whose wedding?"

The queen looked shocked. "Why, yours and Daniel's of course."

The princess found this rather comical. It wasn't that she didn't want to marry Daniel, but the queen was getting a little ahead of herself.

"I didn't know we were engaged," the princess said.

"Well, not yet," the queen said. "But you don't think you'll remain single your whole life?"

"Well, no but—" The princess was cut off.

"Do you intend to marry anyone else?" inquired the queen.

"Well, no but—" Karielle was interrupted.

"Do you think Daniel will remain single?

"Well, no but—" The princess was cut off.

"Do you think Daniel intends to marry anyone else?"

"Well, no but—" Karielle was interrupted.

"Then it's all settled!" the queen exclaimed. "We'll tie together the wedding and the coronation ceremony! Maybe we should tie Cindy and Andrew's wedding into it, too. Then we'll be killing three birds with one stone! Why not? Mind you, you might not want to have a joint ceremony with your cousin. Maybe we should have a week of celebration, with a coronation, two separate weddings, and a thousand feasts with lots of turkey!"

While the queen was getting herself all worked up, Karielle was trying to stop herself from laughing. She had to admit that a week of celebration with three ceremonies did sound exhilarating. And maybe, just maybe, the old man would show up for the party.

Chapter 29

"**I** think Andrew is going to ask me to marry him," Cindy told the princess when they were alone that day.

Karielle almost laughed. She had already had too much marriage talk with the queen that morning. "Why do you think that?"

"Well," she began, "he looks at me, you know, like Daniel looks at you."

Karielle's eyebrows shot up. "Okay. Do you want to marry him?"

Cindy paused. "Well, yeah. But…"

"But what?" Karielle inquired curiously. "Is it because Andrew has changed so much since he saved you?"

Cindy shook her head. "No, it's not that. I like his change."

Karielle nodded. "I'm glad, because I do, too."

"I'm just thinking about Nathan," Cindy explained.

Karielle raised an eyebrow. "You're debating whether or not to get married and you're thinking about your little brother?"

Cindy laughed. "It might sound strange, but yes. Do you think he'll mind?"

Karielle grinned widely. "I think he'll be thrilled."

Cindy looked at the princess curiously. "Really?" she asked.

"Why not? Andrew's great. He'll get a role model," Karielle replied.

Cindy giggled. "I think it'll be a while before I can imagine Andrew as a role model."

The princess shrugged. "You never know. But I really should be going."

She exited the room quickly and quietly. She wondered what she would do for the remainder of the day. She wasn't going to go back to the queen and discuss her supposed upcoming marriage, she didn't want to be present for Andrew and Cindy's engagement, and Nathan was probably running around the castle. She wasn't so keen on tracking him down. That left Daniel. But then, she didn't really want to find him, either. What if he and Andrew had made plans to propose on the same day? Would it be so bad? Like the queen had said, Karielle wasn't planning on marrying anyone else. For the last few days, she had begun to assume that she and Daniel would marry sooner or later. Still, she hadn't planned on it happening so soon. But if it were to happen, why not right away?

Karielle hadn't worked out any of her problems. Eventually, she decided that it would probably be best to start wandering around the castle aimlessly see what or who she ran into.

The princess wasn't very well acquainted with the castle yet. She supposed that it would come with time. She could find herself from outside, to her quarters, and then to the king's old office, but that was about it. She started down an unfamiliar hallway, wondering what kind of rooms it would lead to. She looked to her right, then left. Mirrors and doors alternated. Inside the doors were rooms that were well-decorated and furnished...

The old man shook his head with a smile as he observed the princess. What was she doing? Didn't she want to end this chapter of her life? He would, if he were her. The exhilaration of the last few months of her life had been so extreme, he would have guessed her to be positively exasperated by it all. He would have wanted to settle down and start a calmer, easier life. Running a country wasn't easy, but it seemed to be easier than driving herself insane with mysteries. But she was hesitant. He didn't get Karielle. But that wasn't so much a surprise, since few could comprehend all that the princess did.

He followed her from a distance, making sure that she didn't spot him. He would reveal himself to her soon, but not now. It was not the time yet. She was not anxious to know who he was anymore, he realized. But it was meant for her to know, and he did what was meant to happen. He did the will of the one he served.

The princess entered another hallway. The old man wondered if she even knew where she was going. Probably not. She was probably wandering aimlessly to avoid the unavoidable, or at least to put it off. This again, he did not understand. He was quite knowledgeable that the girl wanted to marry her prince. Why did the female gender have to be so difficult?

Karielle started down a stairway, and the mysterious man smiled slyly. She did not know where she was headed, but the man knew one fact quite well; he knew where she would end up.

Chapter 30

The throne room sparkled gold. The vane pirate's body had long since been removed, and Karielle was more than grateful. The princess remembered the events that had happened in that room, and they made her shiver. Still, it was not the room, but the evil that had once lurked there in the form of Gresmor, the head pirate.

The bright red carpet flowed beneath her feet, and the princess wondered why her feet had led her here. She moved closer to the throne at the end of the room. It certainly was magnificent. She reached out to touch the glistening gold. It was far larger than her, and on each side of it stood solid gold statues of tiger cubs. She looked above the chair of value and rank to rest her eyes on the picture of a crown containing seven jewels. She gazed at it with curiosity. It was lovely, in a strange way. She wondered if the jewels had any meaning. She reached to run her fingers over the jewels. As soon as she touched the picture of the crown, though, she yanked her hand back. The jewels had instantly sparkled with her touch and began to glow.

"Some things in this nation are hard to understand," a familiar masculine voice intoned, startling Karielle. She turned around to see Daniel examining her closely. She moved away from the throne slowly and took a few steps towards him.

"Hello, Daniel," she said, a thread of uneasiness showing in her voice.

"You know, Karielle..." he started, then paused.

"Go on," she said. The princess had a hunch about what he was going to say next.

"You always were one to be a few steps ahead of your cousin, Andrew," he said slowly.

The princess nodded. "I can't argue with that."

"I just saw him a few seconds ago," Daniel told her.

"And?" Karielle asked. It was a question urging him on.

"He was heading in the direction of Cindy's quarters," the prince explained.

"I can only wonder why," she replied sarcastically.

"And since he's going to get engaged in a few minutes, maybe you'd like to get there first," Daniel told her.

Karielle grinned. She had expected this. All in one day, the Lydeen had been found, and she and Andrew were going to get engaged. "Are you asking me to marry you?"

He smiled crookedly at her. "In a matter of speaking," he responded.

"Perhaps," she answered, teasing him.

"Perhaps you'll marry me?" he asked, his left eyebrow raised.

"Yes," she clarified. "Perhaps."

"What does that mean?" he inquired, his curiosity showing.

"Well," she answered, "what do you think it means?"

He paused before answering. "That really depends. Sometimes it means yes, sometimes it means no."

She grinned at him. "That's accurate."

"So?" he urged her to continue.

"So what?" she asked, playing innocent.

"So would you agree to marry me?" he asked again.

Karielle laughed at him. "Yes, I will marry you," she answered. "Does that make you happy?"

"Why shouldn't it?" he asked, his eyes wide. "I wouldn't have asked if it wouldn't make me happy!"

Karielle giggled. "I guess not." She started to walk toward him slowly, as he did her. Stopping when they were arms length from each other, Daniel could feel her warm breath. He slowly started to inch closer to her. Lost in her beautiful, glistening eyes and perfect pink lips, he reached out and kissed her.

When Daniel pulled away from her, he turned to look at the throne, gazing at it intently. The princess, who was following his eyes, mirrored him as he sauntered over to the throne.

"Don't tell me you're thinking of combining our wedding, Andrew's wedding, and the coronation in a week-long celebration," Karielle said with a smile.

He turned toward her, taking her hand in his. "Actually, I was thinking something like that. How did you know?"

A small laugh escaped her lips. "Your mother mentioned it to me this morning."

"This morning?" he asked. Karielle nodded. "Before we got engaged?"

"Well, you don't think she told me after! It's only been a couple of minutes," she replied.

Daniel paused, contemplating what she had just said. "You're right, though I can't imagine why she would say such a thing." "Maybe she likes getting ahead of herself," the princess suggested. She turned her eyes back to the brilliant, regal throne. She still couldn't believe that one day it would be her right to sit in it to rule Prancera. She would have the right to engage in whatever magic lay in the lands ahead, and she would engage with it. She couldn't believe the life that now lay ahead of her.

"Umm... Karielle," Daniel said, motioning for her to look in the opposite direction, toward the door to the throne room. When she did, she witnessed the most peculiar phenomenon. Tiny white sparkles formed in two corners of the room, and then glided toward each other, congregating in the middle.

"What do you think it means?" Karielle asked. Daniel simply shook his head in bewilderment. The sparkles moved closer and closer together until they coalesced in the shape of a diminutive old man. All at once, the sparkles lit up and disappeared, leaving the old, straggly man with centimetre-thick glasses standing in the room with them.

"Good afternoon?" Daniel greeted, though it sounded more like a question.

The old man laughed in such a way that emphasized his age. "Good afternoon to you, too. You might be wondering what I'm doing here and who I am."

"It did cross my mind to ask," Karielle stated.

The old man gave them a wrinkly grin. "It would, I'm sure, but I'll save you the energy. I'm a messenger, a protector, to the true royals of Prancera from the Higher."

"I'm a bit confused, if you don't mind," Daniel told him.

The man laughed once again. "I don't mind at all. Basically, I'm an angel."

"An angel?" the princess asked.

"Yes, a guardian angel sent by the Higher to protect the royals of Prancera. I have served in that capacity for many generations, and will for many generations yet to come."

"I have never heard of you from any of the ancestry royals," Daniel noted.

"That's quite understandable. I was not required to reveal myself when helping them, but your lives have been much more complicated and adventurous than the others. I needed to show myself," the angel explained.

Daniel nodded slowly. "The vision in the water I saw, what did it mean?"

The man returned his nod. "The strange noises like wind and fire represented the truth that the message came from the Higher himself, who has control over earthquakes and all things in this world. The crown in the water was the message itself. Although you were no longer the heir to the throne, you would still rule Prancera as a royal. And you will, once you marry the princess."

Karielle grinned. "I suppose it all works out in the end."

The old man grinned back at her. "Aye, that it does. I must be leaving you, though, and you may not see me again. But you never know." He winked at them, and was gone in a flash. The sparkles returned in his place, and floated towards the throne, making their home in the jewels depicted in the picture. Neither knew what this meant, but they didn't particular feel the need to find out. The answer would come, in time.

And though the old man had left, the presence of the one he served had not. It would never leave, not in that world or this one.

Epilogue

Ａnd so it was that the queen had her wish. After Karielle and Andrew's parents sailed across the Great Sea, a week of celebration began.

It was not long after her coronation that Karielle realized she would not be able to rule two kingdoms at once, so she sent Cindy and Andrew back to Mayblea to rule those lands for her.

Some time after the ceremony, Karielle noticed one day while in the throne room that the seven jewels that made up the crown began to glow magically. She could only assume that they somehow contained the magic of Prancera.

Karielle never returned to her home in Mayblea, and neither did she ever see the old man again. But in her calmer life, she traveled around Prancera and discovered its great beauty. Accepted by the people of her nation, Karielle soon received full duty and honour.

In the historical books of Prancera, the rule of Daniel the Great and Karielle the Gracious is referred to as the Golden Age, when evil no longer roamed the great plains of Prancera.

When Karielle drowned at the age of fifty-two, her eldest of seven, Andrew, named after her cousin, assumed the rule of Prancera. Her decedents ruled the lands of both Mayblea and Prancera.

Nathan Nelson grew up to be Captain Nelson of Her Royal Navy, fighting off Euriko pirate ships and saving helpless villages for a long time to come. He married at age twenty-two to a Prancera peasant and had three children.

Silently and unseen, the old man remained. Perhaps, just perhaps, if you keep your eyes open, you'll see him someday.

About the Author

Janice Vis is a thirteen-year-old author who lives in Barnwell, Alberta with her three brothers and parents. She attends school at Immanuel Christian School Taber Campus and is in grade eight. At the age of twelve, she decided, with the encouragement of others, to attempt to fulfill her dream of becoming a novelist. After about nine months of writing, that dream has come true. She hopes to continue writing for the rest of her life.

Printed in the United States
141744LV00003B/7/P